# THE APEMAN'S SECRET

THE HARDY BOYS® MYSTERY STORIES

# THE APEMAN'S SECRET

## Franklin W. Dixon

### Illustrated by
### Leslie Morrill

WANDERER BOOKS
Published by Simon & Schuster, New York

Manufactured in the United States of America
10 9 8 7 6 5 4 3

Wanderer and colophon are trademarks of Simon & Schuster

THE HARDY BOYS is a trademark of Stratemeyer Syndicate,
registered in the United States Patent and Trademark Office.

Library of Congress Cataloging in Publication Data

Dixon, Franklin W
The apeman's secret.

(His Hardy boys mystery stories; 62)
SUMMARY: A "monster" who terrorizes Bayport and a
girl who runs away to join a cult are the subjects of
the Hardy boys' sleuthing.
[1. Mystery and detective stories] I. Morrill,
Leslie H. II. Title.
PZ7.D644Ap        [Fic]        79-24906

ISBN 0-671-95530-6
ISBN 0-671-95482-2 pbk.

# Contents

# 1

## Huge Footprints

"We're in luck, Frank!" grinned blond, seventeen-year-old Joe Hardy one evening. "Both easy chairs empty and the TV set all to ourselves!"

"Great!" chuckled his brother. "Just in time to watch the Apeman go ape!"

Frank, who was dark-haired and a year older than Joe, switched on the right channel and the boys settled themselves to watch the exciting weekly "Apeman" program.

The hero of the show was a huge, muscular comic book character with a beetling brow and underslung jaw. Sole survivor of the Neanderthal race of cavemen, he was supposed to have been discovered by a scientist on a remote island and

1

brought to America. Frank and Joe enjoyed the program, and tonight's adventure promised to be a real thriller.

Moments later, both boys looked up as they heard dull clanging sounds and a weird hooting outside.

"What on earth is that?" Joe wondered aloud.

"Can't be a foghorn. We're not that close to the water, even assuming it's foggy offshore."

Joe, who was sitting closer to the television, turned down the volume, and the Hardys listened, mystified. The strange noises seemed to be coming from one side of the house.

"Someone must be in the driveway!" Frank exclaimed. He leaped up and flung open the window. The boys peered out. Something moved in the shadows of the shrubbery at one side of the yard. As the boys strained their eyes to make out the cause, a figure took shape in the moonlit darkness.

"Sufferin' snakes! What's that?" Joe gasped.

The figure was clad in metal and had a skull face! A round, tubular horn like a hunting horn was slung over one shoulder. Occasionally the figure would pause long enough to blow a sinister hoot. From its left wrist hung a bell, which clanged mournfully as it swung to and fro.

"Uh-oh! If I didn't think I was seeing things,"

2

Frank muttered, "I'd say that was the Doom Demon!"

"You're right!" his brother declared.

They were referring to another character well known to comic book fans. But unlike the Apeman, the Doom Demon was a villain, who usually fought against the forces of justice led by Captain Star.

The ghastly-looking figure was coming straight toward the Hardys. Suddenly it stopped short and thrust out the fingers of both hands, as if to zap them with lightning bolts of doom!

Sparks of electricity crackled from its fingertips, and at the same moment the figure let out a yelp of pain!

"*Owwwww!*" cried the Doom Demon, hopping up and down and flapping his hands loosely at the wrists as if he had just burned them on a hot stove.

"Hey! There's something familiar about that voice!" said Joe.

"Just what I'm thinking," Frank agreed. "Let's go out and find out who's putting us on!"

"All right, all right! Calm down!" said the weird metal specter outside. "Can't you take a joke?"

The figure pulled off its skull mask, revealing the chubby-cheeked, double-chinned moonface of a youth their own age.

"Chet Morton!" Joe burst out laughing as the Hardys recognized the masquerader. "We might've known!"

4

"Go ahead and laugh, wise guy!" Chet retorted plaintively. I almost got my fingers fried just then—but you think it's funny!"

"You want to come in for some first aid?" said Frank, "or shall we send out a stretcher?"

"Who needs first aid?" Chet sniffed. "But I might go for some cookies or a piece of your Aunt Gertrude's pie."

"Sorry, pal. Joe and I polished it all off at dinnertime. But come on in, anyhow!"

Their stout friend waddled into the house, looking like a robot from a science fiction movie. His costume and helmet turned out to be made of cardboard covered with aluminum foil.

"What brought this on?" Joe asked, as the Hardys looked Chet over in amused astonishment.

"It's my costume for the comic book party at the Alfresco Disco tomorrow night. Don't tell me you guys have forgotten?"

"Hey, that's right!" Joe snapped his fingers and shot a glance at his brother. "We'd better get cooking on *our* costumes, Frank!"

"How do I look?" said Chet, slipping on his skull mask again and turning around proudly to show himself off from all angles. The horn on which he blew his blasts of doom was made of flexible metal conduit, with a funnel stuck in one end to serve as the bell of the horn.

"The Doom Demon, eh?" said Frank, eyeing the

masquerader with a twinkle. "I'd say the measurements are a little broad, but otherwise not bad."

"What do you mean *not bad*?" Chet complained. "It's a work of genius! I expect to win a prize with this costume!"

"What about those sparks from your fingers, when you went to zap us?" Joe put in. "What's your secret?"

"Aw, it's some battery-powered gadget I bought from a mail-order magic supply company." Chet doffed his mask again and pulled back one sleeve of his costume to show the device strapped to his wrist. "But don't ask me how it works. The thing shocked me silly!"

"You can say that again!" Joe chuckled, causing the fat boy to flush peevishly.

"Better watch it," Frank warned. "Instead of zapping someone, you could wind up electrocuting yourself!"

With his usual good nature, Chet Morton ended by joining in the merriment at his own expense. "Say, what show have you got on?" he added suddenly as his eyes fell on the TV set.

"'The Apeman,'" said Joe. "It's pretty good, too. Come on, pull up a chair!"

"Thanks. I love the show."

The three quickly clued in to the action on screen and were soon absorbed watching the program.

According to the story, the scientist who found the Apeman treated him with special drugs to make him look more human. He became so docile and attached to the scientist and his other friends that people often mistook him for an ordinary, timid, and rather backward person of no account.

But the Apeman hated cruelty of any kind. Whenever he saw crooks or villains do something nasty to a helpless victim, he would fly into a rage. This would change his body chemistry and cause him to revert to the savage state. Then, with bulging muscles and fearsome growls, he would beat up the villains and wreck their criminal plot, much to the delight of the audience. Viewers loved to watch him mop the floor with the "bad guys," and the show had become an overnight hit.

"Uh-oh. Here it comes!" Chet muttered. "Those crooks are really asking for it!"

"And now they're going to get it!" Joe added.

On the screen, the Apeman had just taken a gun away from one crook and squeezed it into scrap metal by clenching his fist. Then he proceeded to toss the villains about like beanbags and wreck the evil masterminds' laboratory before ripping open the manacles that held their two prisoners.

"Hey! Did you hear something outside just then?" Frank murmured to his brother.

Joe shook his head. "What did it sound like?"

"More of the Apeman's growls, but I guess it was just part of the sound effects."

The TV show ended and was followed by a brief "News Update" just before ten o'clock. First there were two or three quick headline reports about the international situation and events in Washington. Then the newscaster went on:

"The prankster who's been masquerading as the Apeman has just made another appearance, this time in a local movie theater."

"Hey, we've been there!" Chet exclaimed as the newscaster named a theater in the town of Shoreham, near Bayport.

"Patrons were terrorized," the reporter continued, "and the theater furnishings, glass partitions, and candy counters were extensively damaged before the culprit fled through a rear exit."

"Some prankster!" Joe said disgustedly.

"Witnesses say the impostor looked exactly like the real Apeman in the popular television show and seemed to have equally large muscles. But both the producers of the show and network officials deny any responsibility for such acts or any suggestion that the strong man who plays the TV role may be implicated in what they call 'such lunatic behavior,'" the newscaster concluded.

"Boy! There's a mystery for you guys to ..." Chet Morton's voice faded as a savage growl reached their ears, followed by deep-throated and angry bellows.

"Jumpin' Jupiter! What was that!" the chubby youth exclaimed, his eyes bugging and his jaw dropping open.

Frank leaped from his chair. "Must be the same thing I heard before, whatever *that* was!"

Joe followed as his brother hurried toward the front door and clicked on the porch light before dashing outside. Chet almost collided with the Hardys as they stopped short.

"Look!" Joe gasped, pointing downward.

*There were huge, bare, muddy footprints on the porch! The prints looked semihuman, with the big toes sticking out at an angle to the smaller toes!*

"Whoever made these must've been standing in one of the flowerbeds!" Frank reasoned.

"Right! The ground's still wet there from the rain this afternoon," Joe agreed. "His feet couldn't have gotten this muddy just from walking on grass!"

Frank darted back inside to get a flashlight. Then the boys hastily checked the flowerbeds and shrubbery around the house. Sure enough, there were similar huge footprints in the damp earth under the window that the Hardys had opened a short time earlier when they first saw Chet in his Doom Demon costume.

"This has to be a joke," Joe said.

9

Frank nodded. "Maybe someone else in our gang is going to that comic book party and decided to give us a preview of his costume, like Chet did."

As the boys started back around to the front of the house, a siren wailed in the distance. The shrill noise grew louder, and there was a sudden screech of wheels as the vehicle rounded a corner not far off.

"Hey! It's coming this way!" Joe exclaimed.

Seconds later, a police scout car drew up to the curb. Its front doors flew open, and two officers leaped out. One pointed his nightstick at Chet.

"There's the nut!" he cried, and both policemen rushed at the startled fat boy.

# 2

## Scraps of Evidence

The officer seemed to expect that Chet would run away or resist arrest. But he was too surprised to do anything except stand there blinking at them with a flabbergasted expression.

"What's this all about?" Frank intervened.

"This joker's been scaring people around the neighborhood!" said one policeman.

His partner added, "Someone phoned headquarters about him—said he was heading over to Elm Street—a nut in a metal suit with a skull mask!"

The red-faced, roly-poly youth began stuttering nervously as he tried to explain his appearance. But the skull mask, which was now hanging loosely around his neck by its elastic cord, did nothing to help persuade the officers of his innocence.

"Wait a second!" Joe cut in. "Chet hasn't been scaring anyone! He's been sitting in our living room, watching TV for the last half-hour or so!"

One of the policemen was about to retort suspiciously. Then his expression changed. Instead of relying on the moonlight and the glow of the nearest street lamp, he pulled out his flashlight and shone it at Frank's and Joe's faces.

"Say! You two are Fenton Hardy's sons, aren't you?"

"That's right," Frank said as they both nodded.

Mr. Hardy had once been an ace detective with the New York Police Department. He had retired to the seaside town of Bayport to operate his own agency and was now nationally famous as a private investigator. Frank and Joe seemed to have inherited their father's sleuthing ability and had solved many mysteries on their own.

"Sorry, fellows," the policeman told the Hardys. "If we'd recognized you right off, it would have saved all this hassle."

"I'd like to know what your friend's doing in that nutty getup," his partner persisted.

"There's going to be a party at the Alfresco Disco tomorrow night," Joe explained. "Everyone's supposed to go dressed up like a comic book character. Chet's going as the Doom Demon, so he came over to show us his costume."

"Couldn't he show it to you in the house? How

come you were out here in the dark with a flashlight?"

"Believe it or not, we heard some strange noises," said Frank. "Only it wasn't a loony in a metal suit, it was a loony with big bare feet."

"Are you kidding?" said the first policeman, giving the Hardys another suspicious scowl.

"Come on! See for yourself," Frank offered.

The wail of the police siren had brought lights flashing on along the street, and several neighbors were peering out of their doorways to discover the cause. One of the officers went off to deal with the situation and quiet any feelings of alarm among the neighbors, while the other examined the footprints on the Hardys' front porch.

"They look phony to me," he commented. "Nobody's *that* flatfooted!"

"I think he's right, Frank," Joe agreed after a closer inspection.

The older Hardy boy nodded thoughtfully. "Even one of those Bigfoot critters out West would have *some* bulges on his feet and a *slight* arch. These look flat as a pancake!"

"I'll bet the same person who's responsible for these prints made that phone call to headquarters about Chet!" Joe exclaimed.

"That figures," said the policeman. "The whole thing's probably a practical joke."

The two officers soon drove off, and Chet

started home to the Morton farm in his jalopy, which he had left parked down the street in order to take the Hardys by surprise.

Next morning the telephone rang while the boys were at the breakfast table. Frank answered and heard his father's voice come over the line.

"How's everything on Elm Street, Son?"

"Great, Dad! We had a little excitement last night, but I guess someone was just spoofing us."

Frank briefly described the mysterious events. Mr. Hardy, too, was inclined to ascribe them to a practical joker. But he urged his son to take no chances and to keep the alarm system on at night, in case any criminal he had sent to jail might have been released recently and was looking for an opportunity for revenge.

"Sure, Dad," Frank said. "How about your own case?"

"I can't tell you much about it over an open phone line," the detective replied, "but it's part of a major government investigation. Looks like it may keep me on the move for quite a while yet. Meantime, a friend has consulted me about a case that I'm just too busy to handle. How would you and Joe like to take over?"

"You bet! Let me get him on the other phone so we can both hear the details."

At an urgent signal from Frank, Joe hurried from

the table to listen in on the upstairs extension.

"As you boys know, a lot of my investigative work is done for insurance companies," Mr. Hardy began. "One of those companies is headed by a man named Paul Linwood."

"We've heard you speak of him," said Joe. "Lives in Shoreham, doesn't he?"

"That's right. He has a pretty young daughter named Sue. Unfortunately, a few nights ago there was a bitter family quarrel. The upshot was that Sue ran away from home."

"Has Mr. Linwood heard from her since then?" Frank asked.

"Not a word. But he has a hunch she's joined this odd religious cult called the Children of Noah. Ever heard of it?"

"Sure! We've seen 'em lots of times in Bayport and other towns around here," said Joe. "They hold sidewalk demonstrations."

"They wear white robes," Frank added, "and the guys in the cult shave their heads."

"That's the outfit," Fenton Hardy confirmed. "The cult is primarily composed of young people. So I thought you and Joe might stand a better chance of getting a line on Sue than Sam Radley, my regular operative. Want to give it a whirl?"

"You bet, Dad!"

"Good! I suggest you contact Linwood either at

15

his home or at the Argus Insurance Company, which is also in Shoreham. Call me tomorrow and let me know the score."

Frank jotted down the telephone number at which the detective said he could be reached, then the boys returned to the breakfast table to finish their bacon and eggs. Afterward, they headed out to their laboratory over the garage to finish their costumes for the disco party that evening.

"Did one of you take that cardboard box off the back porch?" their Aunt Gertrude asked as the boys passed through the kitchen.

"No, Aunty," said Joe.

"Well, it was there last night," she said sharply. "I set it out there just before Laura and I went to our club meeting. Don't try to tell me that box got up and walked away by itself."

"We wouldn't dare, Aunty!" Joe grinned.

"You'd better not, young man. And don't let me catch you being funny at my expense, either, not if you want any of the devil's food cake I'm making for dinner tonight!"

"You win. I'll be good!"

Miss Hardy, tall, thin, and tart-tongued, was Fenton Hardy's unmarried sister. Despite her scolding, tut-tutting manner, she was utterly devoted to her two nephews and was also, in Chet's expert opinion, the best pastry cook in Bayport.

"The box must be around somewhere," Frank said helpfully. "We'll look for it."

"I wish you would," Aunt Gertrude said. "I was going to pack some things in it and put them up in the attic."

The boys went outside and when they returned a minute or two later, Frank was holding the missing cardboard box.

"Is this it?"

"Well, I declare! You've found it!" Miss Hardy's pleased smile gave way to a cluck of annoyance as he handed her the box and she saw what had happened to it. "Drat! Someone's torn off the two main flaps. Now I can't close it properly!"

Seeing the slight frown on her nephew's face, she added, "Oh, don't think I'm blaming you, Frank! It was good of you to find it for me. Thank you, dear. Where was it, by the way?"

"Someone tossed it over the back fence. What puzzles me is what happened to those flaps." Frank scratched his head, then exclaimed, "Wait just a minute!"

Turning on his heel, he strode down the porch steps and out to the garbage can, which was standing by the back fence. He took off the cover.

"What in the world ..." Joe started to say, then broke off as Frank fished two rectangular pieces of brown corrugated cardboard out from among the

17

contents of the can. Both were stained and bent.

They were obviously the missing box flaps, and from each one, somebody had cut out a large piece in the shape of a semihuman footprint with the big toe protruding at an angle!

"Well, I'll be a monkey's uncle!" Joe gasped. "So that's how our caller made those phony footprints last night!"

"Right." He pressed the cutouts into the mud of the flowerbed and then used them while they were still muddy to print the tracks on the front porch."

"Smart detective work! What gave you the idea?"

"It occurred to me all of a sudden that the flaps would be about the right size for making the footprints," Frank replied. "But what I'd like to know is whether the guy who did it was trying to be funny or trying to scare us!"

The Hardy boys continued to discuss the mystery that morning as they worked on their party costumes. Frank was going as a champion of justice called the Silver Streak, and Joe as his sidekick known as the Whippersnapper.

Immediately after lunch, they set out for Shoreham in their sleek yellow car. The Argus Insurance Company was located in a large modernistic office building in the main business section of town. The Hardys found a parking spot on a nearby side street, entered the lobby, and gave their names to the receptionist.

Is Mr. Linwood expecting you?" she asked.

"Yes, we phoned for an appointment," Frank said.

Moments later they were escorted to his office. Paul Linwood proved to be a heavyset man with slightly graying hair and handsome features. He greeted the boys with a hearty smile and handshakes, but his gnawing grief became evident as he related the events that had led his daughter to run away from home.

"I'd give anything if I could take back the harsh words that passed during our family quarrel," he confided, pacing back and forth. "I'm afraid I lost my temper, and so did Sue. Perhaps I've been too strict a parent, I don't know. She accused me of trying to run her life. The whole thing ended in a shouting match. Sue walked out and slammed the door, and that's the last we've seen of her."

"Does she have her own car?" Frank inquired.

"Yes, but it's in the repair shop for a transmission overhaul, so she was driving one of our two family cars. The police found it yesterday, parked near a warehouse in the harbor area. There was a note under the windshield wiper, asking them to return it to me."

"Does she work or go to school?"

"She just graduated from Shoreham High a few weeks ago. Her mother and I were hoping she'd go on to college in the fall, but Sue wanted no part of it. Actually, that was one of the things we quarreled about."

"Have you talked to any of the girls she goes around with?" Joe put in.

Mr. Linwood nodded glumly. "We know most of her friends, but apparently Sue hasn't been in touch with any of them."

"Does she have a boyfriend?" Frank asked.

"Yes, a nice lad named Buzz Barton. He's a year or two older than Sue. She had a spat with him, too, the same day as our family quarrel. No doubt that put her in a bad mood and had something to do with her running away—but let me hasten to add, I'm not blaming Buzz for what happened, not for one moment."

"What about this Children of Noah cult?" Frank went on. "Dad said she might have joined it."

"Yes, Sue brought home some brochures and messages they handed out. She seemed to take it all quite seriously. I called it a lot of nonsense, which naturally didn't help matters any."

Joe said, "Suppose you're right, sir, about Sue joining the cult. Any idea where she'd go?"

"The cult owns a converted cruise liner, which their leader, Noah, calls his *Ark*. They keep it anchored offshore, and that's where all the new members are sent."

Linwood added with a gloomy sigh, "Unfortunately the young people aren't allowed to have any contact with their parents, and since Sue's eighteen, she's old enough to do as she chooses. That's why your father thought you fellows might be able to find out more than an older detective."

"We'll certainly try, sir," Frank assured him.

The Hardys left after promising to let Mr. Linwood know immediately if they learned anything about his daughter's whereabouts.

Outside, Frank took the wheel of their car, and Joe slid in beside him.

"Any ideas on how we should tackle this case?" Joe asked as they pulled away from the curb.

His words were drowned out by a loud explosion! Almost at the same moment, their car lurched crazily out of control!

# 3

## Sneak Attack

Frank grabbed the wheel tightly and slammed on the brakes. The car skidded to a noisy halt. A driver behind them honked angrily and swerved out of the way to avoid a collision. But an instant later in passing, he apologized with a wave of his hand as he saw their flat front tires.

"Blowout!" Frank called to his brother in disgust.

The engine had stalled, due to the abrupt stop. Frank revved it back to life and pulled over to the curb. Then the Hardys got out to inspect the damage.

Almost at once Joe spotted a good-sized nail protruding between the treads of the right front tire. "That's what caused one of them," he announced.

"But would two blowouts make that loud an explosion?"

"No way!" Frank declared. Frowning, he retraced their course.

In a few moments he came back, holding what looked like scraps of reddish paper. "There's the answer."

Joe took one of the fragments from his brother for a closer examination and immediately caught on. "A firecracker!" he blurted.

"Right. Someone stuck it in our exhaust pipe. When we started up, the hot exhaust made it explode."

"Which means that nail in the front tire was no accident, either!"

Frank nodded gloomily. "Either someone does not like us in Shoreham, or somebody must have trailed us here from Bayport."

"Maybe the same joker who tried to scare us with those phony growls and footprints last night."

"Could be."

The Hardys got a jack and lug wrench out of their car trunk and dismounted the left front wheel. They found it had been punctured by two nails exactly like the one Joe had noticed in the right front wheel.

"Neat job," Frank said, gritting his teeth. "Whoever did it must have propped them right into place between the tire and the pavement, so the first turn of the wheel would be sure to cause a puncture."

"And we didn't even spot anyone keeping us under surveillance," Joe fumed. "From now on, we'd better watch our step!"

Since they had only one spare tire, Joe wheeled the left flat they had just removed to a nearby gas station to have the tire repaired. Meanwhile, Frank switched the other front wheel with the spare.

Presently Joe came back with the patched and inflated tire. "Hey, the Children of Noah are putting on a demonstration in Franklin Square!" he reported. "Want to go have a look?"

"You bet! This may be a good chance to make contact with them!"

As soon as the Hardys had the wheel remounted, they locked the car and headed for Franklin Square on foot. Even from a block away, they could see the demonstration going on. The white-robed figures were chanting and clapping and rattling tambourines while several others played guitars and recorders.

"What's that song they're singing?" Frank wondered aloud.

"Search me," said Joe. "I'm not even sure you'd call it singing!"

While most of the cultists, or "culties" as people often called them, were chanting, others handed out brochures and mimeographed sheets to the onlookers, including the Hardys. The brochures told about the cult and its leader, Noah. The mimeographed sheets announced that the young people who belonged to the cult could be hired for odd jobs by the day, and it also listed the hourly rate for different kinds of work.

The culties stopped chanting long enough for one shaven-headed youth to step forward and shout at the onlookers. "The old world of darkness and hate is passing away, and those who serve it will be destroyed!" he warned. "A storm of wrath shall sweep them away forever! Only the peace-loving Children of Noah will be saved to start a new world!"

He urged everyone listening to join the cult. Then the chanting and clapping and rather tuneless music began again. The culties who had passed out brochures now moved through the crowd, holding out tin cups for money offerings.

Afterward, as the demonstration ended and the crowd started to break up, Frank and Joe made their way closer to the group of white-robed cultists.

"We'd like to know more about becoming Children of Noah," Frank said to the shaven-headed youth who had given the speech.

The boy scowled at the Hardys. "Why?"

"We were interested in what you had to say," Joe replied. "If we're going to join your cult, we'd like to hear more about it."

Instead of looking pleased, the youth turned to a couple of his companions. They whispered together and shot suspicious glances at the Hardy boys.

Finally, the youth said to Frank and Joe, "Okay, we'll be happy to tell you all about Noah and his wonderful message to the world. Our beloved leader is always happy to welcome new children into our family. We may even take you out to the *Ark* later. Have you heard about our *Ark?*"

"Sure," Joe nodded. "It's that converted cruise liner that your new members live on, isn't it?"

"Yes, it's anchored offshore. There'll be a boat going out to it sometime after five o'clock. Do you know where Decatur and Front streets are?"

"Down by the harbor," Frank replied.

"Right," said the shaven-headed cultie. "On one corner is an old empty warehouse. Wait for us there. We'll be down soon."

The Hardys strolled off through downtown Shoreham in the direction of the waterfront. A few blocks beyond Franklin Square they glimpsed the masts of fishing boats and the smokestacks of freighters tied up at the dock. By following Decatur Street to the harbor, they had no trouble finding the warehouse. It was a ramshackle building with

26

broken and boarded windows. Signs announced that it would soon be torn down to make space for a new shipping-office building.

One of the street-level doors was sagging wide open, evidently with a broken latch and hinges. The Hardys went inside and looked around. In the shafts of sunshine slanting through the broken panes were swirling dust motes, and the concrete floor was littered with rubbish.

"Nice waiting room," Joe remarked sarcastically. "Wonder why they wanted us to come here?"

Frank shrugged. "Don't ask me. Maybe the culties gather here before they go back to the *Ark* every evening."

Frank's suggestion seemed to be borne out by several wooden crates that were grouped together as if they had been used as makeshift benches, while on the floor nearby were discarded candy and gum wrappers and empty soda bottles.

The two boys sat down to wait.

Frank looked thoughtful. "Did you notice how they acted at first when we talked about joining the cult?"

"I'll say I did!" Joe responded. "Not exactly what you'd call real friendly. You'd almost think the Children of Noah didn't *want* any new members."

"Another thing—they're supposed to be such a sweet, kindly bunch, and they always talk about

27

loving your fellow humans, but that guy we heard today sounded as if he was mad at the world."

"Maybe what made him mad was seeing us in the crowd."

Frank frowned and pinched his lower lip. "You know, you might just have something there, Joe."

"But what could he possibly have against *us?*" the younger Hardy boy countered.

"Good question. We'll know the answer to that when we find out why he sent us here."

Minutes later, as the Hardys sat waiting and talking, half-a-dozen white-robed figures burst into the warehouse. All were shaven-headed youths. One was the street preacher they had talked to.

"Now you're going to tell us why you *really* want to join the Children of Noah!" he blurted.

The Hardy boys sprang to their feet.

"What're you talking about?" Frank demanded boldly.

"You know what I'm talking about! You came to spy for the fuzz!"

"You're the sons of that big-shot detective, Fenton Hardy!" another shouted.

"Yeah! And now you're going to get what's coming to you!"

"Now wait a minute!" Frank started to retort.

"And watch whom you're shoving!" Joe added, stiff-arming one of the culties who tried to push them backward and make them stumble over the wooden crates.

Perhaps the blustering youths had really intended to cross-examine the Hardys. But tempers were flaring too fast. Two or three of the culties reached inside their robes and pulled out spray cans.

"Look out, Joe!" Frank warned. "They're going to squirt us!"

An instant later the Hardy boys were being splattered from all directions! Mustard, catsup, hair spray, shaving cream, and shoe polish shot through the air. Some of the Noah culties had armed themselves with more than one can.

But the Hardys had no intention of offering fixed targets to their enemies. Frank lifted the leader off his feet with a left uppercut, and Joe doubled up another one with a punch to the midriff. Fists flying, the two Bayporters fought their way out of the warehouse.

By the time they reached the doorway, both had snatched spray cans from their opponents. Pausing just long enough for a final squirt at their white-robed tormentors, the Hardys dashed outside.

In the sunshine a block away, they stopped and looked each other over.

"What a mess!" Joe grumbled. "They really did a job on us!"

Despite their anger and embarrassment, the

Hardys could not help laughing at their appearance. Their clothes, faces, arms, and hair were smeared in various colors.

"No use crying over spilled milk." Frank grinned ruefully. "Come on! Let's go home and clean up!"

When they pulled into the driveway on Elm Street and walked into the house, Aunt Gertrude gasped in horror. "My stars! What have you two been up to? Some harebrained club initiation?"

"Guess you could call it a 'cult initiation,'" Joe told her.

"Well, get upstairs this minute and clean up, both of you!"

"That's just where we're headed, Aunty," Frank chuckled and winked at his mother who was sitting in the living room. But he paused on the stairway, suddenly noticing the two women's odd, anxious expressions. "Say, is anything wrong?"

"We've been getting nasty phone calls all afternoon," Mrs. Hardy replied.

"Someone on the line growls and bellows like an animal!" Aunt Gertrude added. "Then the caller threatens that our house will be attacked and smashed by the Apeman!"

# 4

## A Savage Surprise

Frank and Joe were furious at the news.

"What did you do?" Joe exclaimed, clenching his fists indignantly.

"Hung up, of course," his tall, sharp-nosed aunt retorted. "I hope you don't think I had any intention of standing there and listening to such silly nonsense."

"Good for you, Aunt Gertrude!" Frank put in. He was tickled by the thought of any crooked caller being foolish enough to believe he could bully or overawe Miss Hardy with mere words.

Nevertheless, it was plain to see that both she and his mother had been upset by the calls.

"I meant what did you *do* about it?" Joe persisted.

"Did you notify the police or try to get in touch with Dad?"

"Well, yes, dear, I rang up Chief Collig after the fourth call," Mrs. Hardy said. "But of course there wasn't much he could do except promise to have the next one traced, if the caller stayed on the line long enough."

"How many calls were there?" Frank asked.

The two women looked at each other.

"Five, weren't there, Laura?" his aunt questioned, then corrected herself, "No, six!"

"That's right," Mrs. Hardy nodded. "There were two more after I phoned the police chief, but they were both short ones, mostly just those scary animal noises."

Frank punched his fist angrily into his palm. "I wish Joe and I had been here to answer, Mom, instead of that creep upsetting you and Aunt Gertrude!"

"Never mind, dear." His mother patted Frank's hand as he came back down the steps to stand by her chair and try to comfort her. "It was probably just some crank. Dinner will be on the table soon, so you boys go on up and get ready now."

Frank and Joe looked at each other but said nothing within earshot of their mother and aunt. In their room, however, as they peeled off their soiled clothes, Joe turned to his brother. "You suppose the caller was the same guy who made those footprints last night?"

"Definitely! What I'd like to know is whether he's the one who gave us those flat tires and stuck the firecracker in our exhaust pipe."

"And how about those bald-headed Children of Noah setting us up in the warehouse for that spray-can blitz," Joe reminded Frank. "Doesn't it seem like quite a coincidence, the two things happening so close together?"

"Sure does. But when we turned up at their street demonstration, the culties may have recognized us from seeing our pictures in the paper or somewhere," Frank pointed out. "You know, in connection with one of the mysteries we've solved. That would explain the warehouse ambush. What it *doesn't* explain is how they could have known beforehand that we intended to investigate their cult."

"Yes, I see what you mean." Joe frowned. "That geek last night sure couldn't have known—we didn't know it ourselves till Dad phoned us this morning!"

"So where does *that* leave us?"

"In the dark, right where we were to start with!"

After dinner the Hardy boys dressed up in their costumes for the comic book party and set out in their yellow car to pick up their girlfriends. Frank, as the Silver Streak, was sleekly togged in a suit that

Aunt Gertrude had helped him sew together out of a silvery metallic curtain fabric. Joe, wearing a horned cap with bells and carrying a short leather whip, was impishly costumed as the Whippersnapper.

After picking up Frank's blonde date, Callie Shaw, who was going to the party as Tiger Girl, they drove on to the Morton farm. Here they met two other high-school pals, Tony Prito and Biff Hooper, who had stopped by with their girls in Biff's gaudily spray-painted van to give Chet a lift to the party.

"Wow! It's that dazzling defeater of evil, the Silver Streak!" Tony cried as Frank got out of the Hardys' car.

"And don't forget his faithful henchman, the Whippersnapper!" exclaimed Joe with a crack of his whip.

Tony was clad in a green reptilian costume as Lizard Man, while lanky Biff Hooper had shaved his head and touched it up with shiny shoe polish in order to go as a comic book villain named Cue Ball. Their dates were impersonating Serpentella and Lady Vampyra.

Soon Chet came waddling out of the house to join them in his Doom Demon costume, clanging his bell and hooting on his horn, followed by his pixie-faced sister, Iola. She was going in a pointy-headed green costume as the Martian Miss.

34

"Hey, you look terrific!" Joe greeted her, and Iola blushed with pleasure.

The two cars promptly started out for the Alfresco Disco. This was an open-air dance pavilion that had just been erected at Bayport Memorial Park to provide summer entertainment for teenagers and older citizens. The Hardys and their friends parked in a crowded lot near the disco and made their way into the pavilion.

The scene was ablaze with psychedelic lights, and a rock group composed of local high-school talent had already begun playing. The disco area was enclosed by decorative sound baffles shaped like shells. They acted as reflectors and amplifiers on the inside but kept the loud music from disturbing other people outside the area.

"Boy, look at all the costumes!" Biff exclaimed. "It's like a comic book come to life!"

A refreshment stand was selling soda, hot dogs, and hamburgers, and tables had been set up all around the pavilion. The master of ceremonies, dressed as a giant bug, was announcing the numbers and calling out wisecracks about the costumes.

"And now, ladies and gentlemen," he went on, "a new hit that's just zoomed to the top of the charts, called . . ."

His voice was drowned out by a sudden loud bellow, followed by gasps and exclamations from the party goers. A burly figure had entered the

35

disco area between two of the shell-shaped sound baffles.

The newcomer was bulging with muscles and clad in a single furry garment. A dark shock of hair grew low over his craggy forehead, and his heavy jaw jutting out below gave him the look of a primitive humanoid creature.

"Hey, it's the Apeman!" Tony exclaimed.

"Jumpin' Jupiter! What a makeup job!" cried Biff. "Something tells me you just lost the costume prize, Chet! This guy's *perfect*. He looks like the *real* Apeman!"

Even as Biff spoke, the creature opened his mouth and emitted another frightening bellow. Then he scowled and began beating his chest with his fists. The audience and disco dancers burst out laughing and applauded loudly, but the Hardy boys exchanged startled looks.

"Wait a minute!" said Frank, pushing away the table and springing to his feet. "That guy didn't come to compete for the costume prize. I bet he's that nut who terrorized the Shoreham theater last night!"

Frank's guess was immediately confirmed as the Apeman punched his huge fist through the nearest sound baffle! Next moment he was overturning tables, breaking up chairs, and smashing everything within reach! As he spread a trail of destruction

through the Alfresco Disco, he bellowed and growled in savage fury.

The party goers scattered in panic. The rock group, too, fled at his approach, two of them dropping their instruments as they ran. But the Hardys were simmering with anger. They had already been attacked by bullies earlier that day, and they were in no mood to submit tamely to a much worse outburst of vandalism.

"Come on! Let's go stop that creep!" Frank exclaimed.

"You said it! I'm with you!" Joe agreed.

"Hey, w-w-wait!" Chet Morton stuttered. "Are you g-guys out of your minds? That Apeman'll break you up in little pieces!"

"Like fun he will!" said Joe. "He may be strong, but he's not strong enough to beat up all of us!"

"Right! Let's take him!" cried Tony Prito.

"Okay, what're we waiting for?" shouted Biff Hooper.

"Are you—are you sure you know what you're doing?" asked Callie Shaw anxiously, plucking at Frank's sleeve.

"Please be careful!" Iola begged.

"We'll be careful," Frank promised. "You girls stay back out of the way!"

Picking up pieces of broken chairs and any other makeshift weapons they could lay hands on, the Hardys and their pals headed straight toward the

Apeman. Taking heart from their example, other youths plucked up courage and joined them.

The Apeman tried to frighten them off with angry bellows and threatening gestures. Then, seeing their grimly determined faces, he hurled a table at them and went bounding off with apelike leaps.

This time he made his way past the row of sound baffles, heading for the entrance at one end of the disco area. There was a brief wild scuffle among the guests unlucky enough to find themselves in his path. The Apeman hurled and flung them aside. Space cleared for his getaway as if by magic. An instant later he was dashing out of the enclosure.

Seeing him go, some of the youths in the impromptu posse were only too happy to give up the chase. But the Hardys and their friends pressed a hot pursuit.

"Keep going!" Frank urged. "Let's nail that nut while we've got the chance!"

"We're with you!" Tony promised.

They could see the brutish figure disappearing into the darker reaches of the park. Frank, Joe, and their companions fanned out to cut off his escape but soon lost sight of him.

Only a few people were using the park at this late hour, including several couples strolling arm in arm, a cripple on a bench, and an old man walking his dog. The Apeman was nowhere to be seen.

"Guess we've lost him," Joe said after a final look around.

"Never mind, at least we gave him a good workout," said Frank. "Thanks a lot, fellows, for sticking with us."

Returning to the Alfresco Disco, they saw Chet, Iola, Callie, and several more of their friends huddled over a scattering of items on the ground near the entrance.

"No luck?" Chet asked, glancing up as they approached.

"He got away," Joe reported. "What are you looking at?"

"Stuff that got ripped or spilled out of somebody's pocket during that getaway scuffle."

"What's so interesting about it? Anything look valuable?"

"Not exactly, but take a look at this." Chet held up an odd-shaped metal amulet. "Ever seen anything like it before?"

The amulet bore the image of a flying bird with something in its mouth.

As the Hardys examined the object and shook their heads, Iola held up a scrap of paper. "And here's something that should *really* interest you!" she said.

Frank and Joe gasped in surprise as they saw what was written on the paper. *It was the address of their house on Elm Street!*

# 5

## Hot News

"You just found this lying on the ground?" Frank asked with a puzzled glance at Iola.

"Chet found it," she replied.

The chubby youth explained that he had been running along with the posse but had stumbled in his awkward costume and seen the scrap of paper as he fell. "There was enough light over the entrance to see what was written on it. It was your address!"

The paper looked as if it had been torn from an envelope, but no other writing or printing was visible on it.

"If all this stuff was lying together, then it must have come out of the same person's pocket," Joe reasoned.

Iola nodded. "Right! That's what we figured, if it's any help."

"Not much, I'm afraid," Frank replied, "but we'll check it out."

The other items were commonplace objects, including six cents in change, a New York subway token, an ad book of matches, and half a roll of breath mints.

Frank and Joe carefully slipped the objects into one of the small plastic bags they always carried with them for collecting evidence. As they rose to their feet, they heard clapping and several cheers.

"Nice going, fellows!" a man called out.

"Thank goodness someone had spunk enough to chase that dumdum away!" another exclaimed. "He would've wrecked the whole pavilion!"

Much to the Hardy boys' embarrassment, they realized they were being acclaimed as heroes. A TV camera, poised on a cameraman's shoulder, was being trained on them, while an interviewer held out a microphone.

"What made you brave enough to chase after such a terrifying monster as the Apeman?"

"I doubt if he was the real Apeman," Frank said mildly. "The person who plays that role in the TV show is probably in California where the television movies are produced."

"You may be right," said the reporter, "but the

42

one we just saw looked scary enough to me!"

"He was strong," Joe added, "but that doesn't mean he's superman. As soon as he realized that people were ready to put up a fight, he ran off."

"Can you tell us exactly what happened?"

The Hardy boys took turns describing their chase. Tony and Biff also put in one or two remarks, and the interview finally ended.

The comic book costume party resumed, but despite the excitement, some of the fun had gone out of the evening. Much to Chet's disgust, a girl dressed as Space Sprite won the costume prize. By ten-thirty, Frank and Joe and their dates decided to leave the party, along with many of their friends.

Privately, the Hardys were relieved at the prospect of going home early. Both boys were worried that the same frightening caller who had harassed their mother and aunt that afternoon might bother the two ladies again while they were alone in the house at night.

After taking Callie home first, they drove Iola out to the Morton farm. Chet had already arrived and shucked his costume. Now he was sitting alone in the living room watching television, Mr. and Mrs. Morton having gone to bed.

The plump youth came out on the porch after the Hardys' car pulled up in front of the house. Just as Joe was about to see Iola up to the door, Chet waved excitedly. "Come on in!" he called. "They're going to have something about the disco on the 'Eleven O'Clock News'!"

Frank and Joe accepted the invitation and went inside with Chet and Iola.

Sure enough, the newscaster was just saying, "And now we have a late report from the Alfresco Disco at Bayport Memorial Park, which was raided tonight by the same vandal who's been posing as that television character, the Apeman!"

Not only were there shots of the disco party, in which the Hardys and Mortons recognized a number of their friends in costume, but Frank and Joe were shown close up being interviewed, along with Tony and Biff.

"My hero!" Iola giggled, seizing Joe's arm.

"Oh, it was nothin', ma'am," he quipped. "Actually we were just after the Apeman's autograph. We didn't know he was a fake."

More interesting to the Hardys than their own interview was the videotape sequence showing the weird vandal. The television news team had been sent to the disco to do a story on the comic book costume party. They had arrived just in time to film the Apeman impostor live, in the very act of carrying out one of his wrecking raids.

By using a telephoto lens, the cameraman had been able to get some remarkable close-up shots of the mysterious raider.

"Boy, he sure seems like the real McCoy," Chet exclaimed.

"You said it!" Joe chimed in. "We just saw Apeman on TV last night, remember? This guy looks so much like him, I bet he could take over the same role in the show and no one would spot the difference."

Almost as if the boys' conversation had been heard in the television studio, the newscaster went on, "By the way, in case any of you out there are harboring any suspicions about the TV character, one of our network reporters in California has just been in touch with him by telephone. He confirms that the real Apeman is, indeed, at his home near Hollywood."

Nevertheless, with his shaggy mop of black hair growing low over his forehead, his brutal features and undershot jaw, the vandal on videotape might have been a twin brother of the character he was impersonating.

"It's an amazing resemblance, all right," said Frank. "Somebody must have done an expert make-up job on him. And there's no way those big muscles could've been faked!"

"Talking about expert makeup jobs," Joe put in, "it's too bad you didn't win anything tonight with your Doom Demon costume, Chet. It rated a prize."

"I think so, too," Iola sympathized. "In that

costume, Chet looked a lot more convincing than the Space Sprite."

"A lot more solid, anyhow," Frank said with a twinkle.

"But not nearly as cute," Joe teased. Then he grinned as Iola playfully stuck out her tongue at him.

"Aw, who cares," said Chet, heaving himself up out of the rocking chair he had been occupying. "Cartooning's where the big money is! And that's what I'm going into from here on."

"Don't tell us you're taking another mail-order course?" Frank inquired half jokingly.

"You bet! It's called *The Seven-Day Way to Fame and Fortune in Cartooning.* I'm only halfway through the book, and I've already dreamed up a terrific superhero for the comic books! Wait'll I show you."

Chet bustled upstairs to his room and came back with a page of drawings and balloons laid out in cartoon panels. They portrayed a character called Muscle Man. The Hardys could see that Chet had worked hard on his creation, but privately they felt that he had a long way to go.

"I think you should call him *Muscle Head,*" Joe commented with a straight face.

"Okay, wise guy," Chet retorted good-natured-ly, clamping a playful headlock on the younger

46

Hardy boy. "Any more cracks and I'll muscle *your* head!"

"Never mind him, stick with it, Chet," Frank said encouragingly. "Maybe you're onto something."

On the way home from the Morton farm, Joe, who was at the wheel, noticed headlights steadily behind them in the rearview mirror. As he watched, they suddenly went off, as if the driver realized he had been observed.

"Think we have a shadow," Joe muttered.

"Maybe the same one who tailed us to Shoreham this afternoon," Frank suggested.

"Could be!"

Rounding a bend, Joe pulled off into a side road, hoping to take their follower by surprise as he passed. But no car appeared.

"Maybe I was imagining things," he said, feeling slightly foolish.

Much to the Hardy boys' alarm, they found a police car stationed outside their house on Elm Street. "Just keeping an eye on things," said one of the officers. "The ladies'll tell you about it."

Rushing inside, Frank and Joe found their mother and Aunt Gertrude having tea in the living room in their bathrobes. Both were in a nervous state.

"What's happened?" Frank asked anxiously. "More calls?"

"Worse!" snapped Gertrude Hardy. "We heard bellowing outside. Then we saw this awful face at the window, like that Apeman on television!"

"I'm afraid I screamed," Mrs. Hardy confessed. "Then he smashed his fist through the glass!"

# 6

## A Sticky Shadow

"Did the nut try to climb in?" Joe asked his mother and Aunt Gertrude.

"No, thank heavens! But I admit I was terrified," Mrs. Hardy replied. "Not Gertrude, though. She ran out to the kitchen and grabbed a rolling pin!"

"I'd have used it on him, too!" Miss Hardy asserted with a grim look in her eye.

"I'll bet you would've," Frank said admiringly. "But how about the fake Apeman? What was he doing—just standing there, glaring in?"

"We really don't know," the boys' mother admitted. "While Gertrude was going for the rolling pin, I was phoning the police."

"By the time I got back from the kitchen, the brute

was gone," Miss Hardy took up the story. "When the police arrived, they couldn't find hide nor hair of him. I think he realized if he tried any more funny stuff, he was asking for real trouble!"

"If he didn't, he was no judge of character," Joe agreed, repressing a smile. "Boy, when you go on the warpath with a deadly weapon like that rolling pin, Aunt Gertrude, you could sure flatten a lot more than a piecrust!"

"Flattery will get you nowhere, young man!" Miss Hardy retorted, but the stern look on her sharp-featured face was partly betrayed by the pleased twinkle in her eyes.

Both ladies looked somewhat calmer now that the boys were home and had heard the details of their frightening ordeal.

"Is the alarm system on?" Frank asked.

"It is now," said his mother. "I turned it on right after I phoned the police. We should have switched it on as soon as you two left, but we neglected to do so. From now on, we'll know better! How was the party, by the way?"

"Exciting," Frank said dryly.

"We got a look at the Apeman, too," Joe added. "In fact we chased him!"

"For goodness' sake, what happened?" Mrs. Hardy inquired. Forgetting their own upsetting experience, the ladies now looked concerned over the boys' adventure that evening.

"Give us a full report," said Gertrude Hardy, her detective instincts aroused.

Frank and Joe told how the mysterious wild man had suddenly appeared at the Alfresco Disco and threatened to smash up the dance pavilion, until they had driven him off with a counterattack.

"We even got interviewed on television," Joe concluded. "We saw ourselves on the 'Eleven O'Clock News' out at Chet's place."

"Oh, dear! I don't like that bit about our address turning up on the piece of paper your friends found on the ground," Mrs. Hardy fretted.

"It may be nothing to worry about, Mom," Frank tried to reassure her. "It could have fallen out of the pocket of somebody in our high-school crowd."

"Sure, that's the likeliest answer," Joe agreed. "Or maybe someone who intends to get in touch with us for detective work. The only really unusual thing is this coin or amulet."

Holding the metal disk by its edges so as not to smear any possible fingerprints, Joe plucked it carefully from the plastic bag in which he and Frank had placed the various objects.

Gertrude Hardy frowned shrewdly at the picture stamped on the curious amulet. "That's a dove bearing an olive branch!" she declared.

Frank snapped his fingers. "Of course! From the Bible story of Noah's Ark!"

"Actually, in the Book of Genesis," Miss Hardy

corrected, "the dove flew back to the Ark carrying an olive *leaf* in its beak. But most folks call it an olive branch."

"The important thing," said Joe, "is the Noah angle." He glanced at his brother. "Do you suppose there's any connection between the Children of Noah cult and this nut who's impersonating the Apeman?"

Frank shrugged, knitting his brows in a puzzled expression. "You've got me there. But it's an angle we should start looking into."

Before turning in for the night, the Hardy boys took the plastic bag to their laboratory over the garage to check the assorted objects for fingerprints. But the dusting powder failed to bring out a single print that was clear enough for identification purposes.

Next morning, soon after breakfast, the telephone rang. Frank answered and heard a breezy, fast-talking voice.

"You one of the Hardy boys?"

"Yes, I'm Frank Hardy. Who's calling, please?"

"Micky Rudd. I'm the editor and publisher of Star Comix. Maybe you've seen some of our comic books."

"I sure have. A lot of kids in Bayport read them," Frank said with a slight chuckle. "What can I do for you, Mr. Rudd?"

"You and your brother open for any investigative work right now?"

"You bet! Just what would you like us to investigate?"

"I'd rather not talk about it over the phone. Could you come to my office in New York?"

"How soon?"

"What about today—after lunch?"

Frank caught his breath then grinned wryly and glanced at his watch. Micky Rudd was obviously a man who believed in wasting no time. "Yes, sir, I guess we could make it," Frank agreed.

"Fine!" Rudd rattled off the address of the Star Comix editorial offices and added, "See you at one, buddy!"

Frank heard the receiver crash down at the other end of the line. He hung up and turned to Joe with a slightly dazed smile.

"Wow!"

"What was that all about?" the younger Hardy boy asked.

"We just got consulted by the publisher of Star Comix. He wants us to come to New York and tackle some kind of detective case."

"Uh-oh!" Joe gave a low whistle. "Wonder if it has anything to do with this phony Apeman vandal?"

"Sounds like a good guess. The Apeman's a Star

Comix character. Whatever's up, we're going to have to step on it. We're due in the publisher's office at one o'clock!"

Before leaving, the Hardy boys phoned their father to report developments. But they could get no answer at the number he had given them.

They also stopped in Shoreham to see Paul Linwood and tell him about their encounter with the Children of Noah the previous afternoon.

"You mentioned that Sue had a boyfriend," Frank added.

"Yes, a chap named Buzz Barton."

"Since the culties know our faces, we may need an operative they *don't* know. Do you suppose he'd help us?"

"I'm sure he would!" the insurance company president declared. He promised to arrange a meeting when the Hardys returned from New York.

The weather was perfect for their trip, a cool, sunny summer day. Frank and Joe enjoyed the ride as their car whizzed along the turnpike. Then Joe noticed his brother watching the rearview mirror.

"What's the matter? Do we have company?"

"Could be. A brown station wagon's been on our tail ever since we got on the turnpike."

"Did you notice it when we left Shoreham?"

"Nope. But to tell you the truth, I wasn't paying much attention."

"Can you make out the driver?" Joe asked.

"Not very well. Let's see if I can nudge him out in the open."

Frank tried slowing down, but the only result was a series of honks from impatient drivers. The brown station wagon continued to keep its distance. Traffic was heavy, and most of the time the driver managed to maneuver so that other cars screened him from the Hardys.

At last the Manhattan skyline came into view, dominated by the Empire State Building and the twin towers of the World Trade Center. When the boys entered the city, Frank drew over to the curb to watch for their shadow.

But the brown station wagon failed to appear. Either it had peeled off from the flow of traffic at an earlier exit or else had sneaked past unseen behind some larger vehicle, like one of the huge tractor trailers that thronged the turnpike.

"How do you like that? He gave us the slip!" Frank muttered in annoyance. "Oh well, maybe I was just imagining things."

"That's what you said last night," Joe pointed out wryly. "Do you imagine things that often, or is twice in twelve hours just a coincidence?"

"When you put it that way, anything's possible. Let's keep a sharp lookout at all times. If we *are* being tailed, that's the one way to trap our shadow."

Though neither mentioned it, both boys recalled the blowouts their car had suffered yesterday in Shoreham and the firecracker that had been stuck in their exhaust pipe. That episode, too, seemed to indicate they were under surveillance. If so, their shadow was not only malicious but persistent.

After leaving their car in a midtown parking garage, Frank and Joe made their way to Star Comix's editorial offices in Rockefeller Center. Its walls were decorated with full-length color pictures of the company's various superhero characters: the Apeman, the Silver Streak, Serpentella, the Doom Demon, and others.

Micky Rudd proved to be a rangy, bald-headed man who seemed to live in a constant state of excitement. After inviting the Hardys to sit down, he paced about the office. "I saw you fellows on television last night," Rudd began, "so I don't need to tell you about this nut who's impersonating the Apeman."

Frank nodded. "We saw him at the disco."

"Then you know he's dangerous! That's why I'm hoping you two will take the case. I want you to hunt him down before he blows his top completely and does something really serious!"

# 7

## Muscle Men

"What made you call on us, Mr. Rudd?" Joe asked.

"As I say, I saw you on television last night. That's what made me think of you. But that's not the *only* reason; no, indeed!" Micky Rudd paused to flash a brilliant smile at the Hardys, as if he were spotlighting them in the full, dazzling glare of his hundred-kilowatt personality. "People all over the country have heard of the Hardy boys and their famous dad! They *trust* you. If they read that Star Comix has asked you two to find this phony Apeman, they'll know it's a real mystery case!"

Rudd whipped a vivid blue silk handkerchief out of his breast pocket to dab the perspiration from his forehead.

Frank frowned thoughtfully. "Are you implying that otherwise some people may think the raids and the vandalism are just a dirty trick to get some free publicity?"

"Of course! What else?"

"Seems a bit farfetched, doesn't it?"

"Sure, it does to us because we know it's not true. But not to the general public, it doesn't. They think if we're in the comic book business, we must be crazy to start with!"

Joe repressed a grin. "You'd *have* to be crazy to damage your own starring character."

"Right!" Rudd explained. "That's just the point. All this monkey business could wreck the public image of the *real* Apeman. If folks keep hearing how this fake Apeman goes around threatening people and wrecking property, some of that unpleasantness could rub off on our copyrighted comic book character. It could ruin the appeal of his television show!"

Rudd pulled out his handkerchief and mopped his forehead again as he resumed pacing about the office.

"So you assume that's the impostor's motive?" Frank asked.

Rudd shrugged helplessly. "Who knows? The nut must hate *somebody,* the way he keeps smashing things up!"

"Can you think of anyone who might have a spiteful grudge against Star Comix?"

The bald-headed editor-publisher flung himself into his desk chair and screwed his face into a thoughtful scowl. "Well, let's see. There's an artist named Hamp Huber, who probably doesn't like Star Comix too well right now."

"Why not?"

"He used to draw our Apeman comic book, but last month I fired him."

"How come?" put in Joe.

"Oh...we had various differences. The main thing was, we couldn't depend on him to deliver the work on time."

"This fellow Huber was a free-lance artist?"

Rudd nodded. "Most of our comic books are done that way, by free-lance artists and writers who work at home. The guys you see working at drawing boards here in the office mostly just do coloring or make changes when we discover a goof in the pictures or balloons."

Frank said, "Give us Huber's address, please, and we'll check him out."

"Any other possible suspects?" Joe added.

Rudd scratched his jaw. "Well, maybe I shouldn't mention him, but there's Gil Ostrow."

"Who's he?"

"The editor in chief of Galaxy Comics. That's our

59

main competitor. From what I hear, Gilly's pretty jealous about the big hit our Apeman character has made on TV."

"Is Galaxy located here in New York City?" Frank inquired.

"Yes. A few blocks up on Madison Avenue." Rudd added the address to Hamp Huber's name and address and handed the slip of paper across his desk to the older Hardy boy.

"Is there any chance the impostor may have some connection with the TV show?" Frank went on.

Micky Rudd thought for a moment, then shook his head doubtfully. "I can't think of anyone in the television end of things who'd be mad enough at us to pull such a trick. But the guy to talk to about that is Vern Kelso."

"He's a television executive?"

"Yes, at the Federated Broadcasting System. That's the network that carries 'The Apeman.' Vern and I worked together to develop the show, and then he helped sell it to the top brass at FBS."

The Hardys looked at each other to see if either had any more questions, then rose and shook hands with the bald-headed publisher.

"Okay, Mr. Rudd," said Frank. "We'll do our best to find out who's behind all this trouble."

"Good! I'm counting on you Hardy boys!"

From Rockefeller Center, the two young sleuths

walked north up Fifth Avenue toward Central Park. The street was fronted by fashionable shops, and on the right loomed the imposing gray spires of St. Patrick's Cathedral.

"What did you make of Rudd?" Joe asked his brother as they turned toward Madison Avenue.

Frank grinned dryly. "I'd say he's quite a character himself. But underneath all that fast talk, I get the impression he's really worried over this nut who's on the loose, and maybe not just about the public relations angle, either!"

"Same here," Joe agreed. "Once or twice he looked downright scared, almost as if he thought that fake Apeman might come after *him!*"

Although they had no appointment, the editor in chief of Galaxy Comics agreed to see the Hardy boys as soon as he heard who they were. He turned out to be a gnomelike man with a wild shock of rusty, graying hair that stuck out in all directions.

As they shook hands with him in turn, Frank and Joe exchanged hasty glances. The same thought was passing through both boys' minds. If Gil Ostrow really *was* behind the malicious vandalism, at least they could be sure of one thing; he certainly wasn't impersonating the Apeman himself. He was not big enough.

"Sit down, fellows," Ostrow said. "Tell me what brings the Hardy boys to Galaxy Comics."

Frank explained that they were trying to find the mysterious vandal who had been posing as the Apeman. Since Galaxy Comics was the main competitor of the Apeman comic books' publisher, it was natural to include Galaxy in their investigation. Frank tactfully named no names, but Gil Ostrow's immediate response was a sarcastic smile.

"So Micky Rudd sicced you on me, did he?" Ostrow chuckled contemptuously. "That figures!"

"Why do you say that, Mr. Ostrow?" Joe asked.

"Listen, Son! Rudd and I have been feuding for years. That big mouth would stoop to anything to do me a bad turn!"

"Then you deny that you'd have any reason to try and make people sore at the Apeman character?"

"Of course I deny it! Why should I want to cause the show any trouble? I think it's great having a comic book character on television. The more the better! It's good for our business!"

"If you're telling us the truth," said Frank, "why should Mr. Rudd try and throw suspicion on you?"

"I just told you, we've been feuding for years. He probably didn't mention that we sell twice as many comic books as Star Comix does." Ostrow hesitated a moment, studying his fingernails, then looked up with a cold smirk at the Hardys. "Let me put it this way, boys. I'll just quote you a remark that was made to me several years ago by an artist named Archie Frome. Archie's dead now, so he won't mind if I repeat it. He said to me once, confidentially, *'That guy Rudd's a real crook!'* End of quote."

"Any idea what he was referring to?" Frank probed.

"I wouldn't even try to guess, Son. I'm not that interested in Rudd's business. I merely quote the remark for whatever it's worth."

Before returning to their car, the Hardys stopped at a coffee shop for hamburgers.

"Look, Frank! Whoever's impersonating the Apeman must be a real muscle-type," Joe reasoned. "Right?"

His brother nodded. "That's for sure. Nobody's *born* with a build like that guy's got. The only way to get a chest and arms that big is by working out with weights for a long period of time. He looked like a pro to me."

"Check! And from what I've read, the favorite spot for body-building enthusiasts in this part of the country is the Olympic Gym. Why don't we go there and see if we can pick up any clues?"

"Good idea!"

The boys looked up the address of the Olympic Gymnasium in the Manhattan telephone directory. It turned out to be located in the basement of an office building in the West Forties, not far from the seedy Times Square area.

The spacious room was filled with young men in

gym trunks who were working out with barbells and tugging rhythmically at the handgrips of weight-lifting machines. The atmosphere reeked of liniment and perspiration.

A powerfully built fellow with one leg in a plaster cast was seated on a bench near the door, enviously watching the exercisers. As Frank and Joe came in and looked around for someone who might give them information, he suddenly exclaimed, "Say! You two are the Hardy boys, aren't you?"

Frank and Joe responded with friendly grins and introduced themselves.

"I *thought* I recognized you," he said. "I saw you on TV last night. I'm Rollo Eckert."

They shook hands.

"Don't tell me you guys are working on the Apeman case?" he inquired.

"The *fake* Apeman case." Frank smiled. "Matter of fact we are. Maybe you can help us."

"Glad to, if I can."

"We'd like to know how many men in this part of the country are near enough to champion class to impersonate the Apeman."

Rollo Eckert looked embarrassed. He hesitated before replying, "'Fraid I can't help you much there. I just don't know the local body builders well enough. Actually I'm from California. I just came east because I was offered a part in a Broadway show. But then I had an accident and broke my leg. So now I can't even go home to California until the lawsuit over the accident is settled."

"Tough break," said Joe with a glance at Frank. Both Hardys felt that Eckert was stalling because he was too polite or cautious to name any names.

"I'll tell you someone who might know, though," Eckert went on helpfully. "A friend of mine, Zack Amboy. He just went into the locker room to dress, but he'll be out in a minute. Zack's a world-class body builder. In fact, he won the title of Mr. Hercules last year. He knows all the guys who pump iron around here."

Presently Amboy emerged onto the floor of the gymnasium, wearing street clothes. He greeted the Hardys enthusiastically when Rollo introduced them.

"Pleased to meet you, fellas! I've heard a lot about you and your old man. Saw you on the television news last night, by the way!"

Although Zack was impressively big and seemed very good-natured, Frank and Joe got the impression that he might not be overly bright.

Eckert told him why the Hardys had come and then went hobbling off on crutches. Zack scratched his head thoughtfully and began counting on his fingers.

"Well, let's see. Come right down to it, I can only think of eight guys who might be able to go around pretending they were the Apeman. Y'understand now, I'm not talking about their faces, just their builds."

Frank said, "If you saw what happened at the disco last night on the TV news, then you also must have seen the faker who impersonated the Apeman.

Zack nodded. "Sure, I got a good look at him. That guy had a great set of muscles! He could win plenty of competitions!"

"Could you give us the names and addresses of those eight body builders you mentioned?"

"Sure thing. I dunno where they all live, but I can get their addresses out of the files."

Amboy went into the office of the gymnasium manager. He soon came out again, holding a slip of paper with the names and addresses. "There you go, fellas."

Frank and Joe thanked him and said good-bye as the manager came over to speak to the strong man. The two boys walked out of the gym and were on their way through the basement corridor toward the stairs when Zack came running after them.

"Hey, there's a call for Frank Hardy!"

Surprised, Frank went back to answer the phone. Joe waited for him and chatted for a minute with Zack, who was on his way out of the building.

Meanwhile, Frank picked up the phone in the manager's office. "Hello," he said but got no response. "Hello! . . . Hello?"

There was still no reply. Frank waited, thinking the party might have been called away from the phone. But after a while he heard a click as the person hung up.

Frank lowered the phone in puzzlement. Suddenly a thought struck him. He put down the receiver and ran out of the gym, only to stop short in dismay.

*Joe lay sprawled unconscious in the corridor!*

# 8

## Sea Signal

Frank knelt down anxiously to examine his brother. Joe's pulse was strong and regular, and his only injury was a bump on the back of the head.

Remembering a first-aid cabinet that he had noticed on the wall of the gym, Frank ran back to fetch a bottle of smelling salts. He waved it under Joe's nose and chafed his wrists. Presently the younger Hardy boy revived and sat up.

"Wow!" Joe rubbed his head and looked around to get his bearings.

"Can you remember what happened?" Frank asked.

Joe recalled chatting briefly with Zack Amboy. After Zack left, he said, he had walked up and down the basement corridor for a bit while waiting for Frank to rejoin him. "Then someone slugged me from behind!" Joe ended ruefully.

"How do you feel? Want to go to a doctor?"

"No, I'm okay. Whoever conked me didn't hit me all that hard. I was just stunned. What about that phone call?" Joe inquired. "Just a trick?"

"Yes, to separate us, so whoever knocked you out could pull his stunt," Frank said angrily. "When I picked up the phone, no one answered. He kept me on the line just long enough to slug you."

"What's the angle?" Joe said and got up on his feet carefully. "Any ideas?"

"Probably a warning to keep our noses out of the Apeman mystery."

"Who do you suppose set us up, one of the musclemen at the gym?"

Frank shrugged. "It's possible. Or it could have been the sneak who's been trailing us."

There was a public telephone on the stairway landing. The boys tried calling their father again and this time got an answer. Fenton Hardy listened to their report with concern, then asked them to read out the list of eight possible suspects that Zack Amboy had provided.

After hearing their names and addresses, the ace detective commented, "They live quite far apart, in three different states. Tell you what. I'll have some of my operatives check them out. That way we can eliminate whichever ones have alibis for last night and the other times the fake Apeman went on a rampage." Mr. Hardy took down the information and added, "In the meantime, you boys watch your step. If what happened to Joe was a warning, you may be in considerable danger!"

"We'll be careful, Dad," Frank promised.

On their way home from New York, the Hardys stopped in a pleasant suburban community called Fair Oaks, where the artist Hamp Huber lived. He was a big, affable man, at least a good match in size for the Apeman's impersonator. Evidently he had been working at the drawing board when the Hardys arrived. His open-necked sports shirt was slightly ink- and-paint-stained.

After sizing Huber up, both boys felt that their best tactic was to be completely frank about the reason for their visit.

"Sure, I'm sore about getting fired by Star Comix," the artist admitted, "but not because I need the job. No good illustrator has any trouble getting assignments these days, and I'm one of the best, if I do say so myself! I've got all the work I can handle."

"Then what's your gripe?" said Joe.

"I've been drawing the Apeman comic book for over two years," Huber said. "I gave it the best I had. I really think I helped build up the character. And now when it all starts to pay off and the Ape-man gets popular on television, do I get a raise or a pat on the back? No, I get fired!"

"We were told they couldn't depend on you to deliver the work on time," Frank said bluntly.

"Baloney! They've been satisfied with my performance these past two years. What's so different now? That's typical of the way Micky Rudd operates!"

"How do you mean?"

"He thinks he's the one-man genius of Star Comix," Huber replied. "Whenever he's afraid that any artist or writer may get too much credit for some character or comic book, right away Rudd finds an excuse to fire him or switch him to another assignment. That's so Rudd can hog all the credit himself!"

Frank hesitated a moment before asking, "Ever hear of an artist named Archie Frome?"

"Sure, he died not long ago. A very talented guy!"

"Somebody told us he called Mr. Rudd 'a real crook.'"

Hamp Huber chuckled heartily. "If old Archie Frome said that, you better believe it!"

"Why?"

"Archie was one of the nicest fellows you'd ever

71

want to meet; warmhearted, always sweet-tempered. I've never heard him say an unkind word about anybody. So if he actually called Micky Rudd a crook, he must've had some mighty good grounds for saying so!"

When they resumed their drive to Bayport, Frank and Joe made another stop in Shoreham, at the Argus Insurance Company offices. It was a few minutes after closing time, and Mr. Linwood brought Sue's boyfriend out to the lobby to meet them.

Buzz Barton was a husky, freckle-faced young man. The Hardys liked him immediately. He was eager to do anything possible to help find Sue Linwood. Like her father, Buzz suspected that she might have joined the Children of Noah.

"But here's the catch," Frank explained. "Joe and I have already had one run-in with the culties and they know our faces. If we're going to find out whether or not Sue's aboard the *Ark*, we'll have to have somebody else act as spy. That's where you come in."

"Leave it to me!" Buzz volunteered. "There's always a group of 'em down around the waterfront just before dinnertime. I'll pretend I want to join. One way or another, I'll get aboard!"

"Good! If she *is* on the *Ark* and the culties make any trouble, Joe and I can meet you out at the ship and bring you both ashore. We have a good fast boat."

"I'll try and call you this evening," Buzz promised, "and let you know the score."

Joe drove the last leg of their trip home. Once again the Hardys had a strong hunch that they were being shadowed but in the busy rush-hour traffic were unable to trap the tail car.

When they arrived home, their mother said that Chet Morton had stopped by during the afternoon. "I told him you'd gone to see the publisher of Star Comix in New York, and he got very excited," Mrs. Hardy added. "I'm not sure why."

"Uh-oh! Three guesses!" groaned Joe with a comical look at his brother.

Frank grinned. "Let's face it. It must have something to do with this new cartooning kick he's on."

Sure enough, their plump pal showed up just as Aunt Gertrude was setting the table for dinner. Chet brought fresh samples of his artistic output. The Hardy boys saw that he had changed the name of his cartoon character from Muscle Man to Captain Muscles.

"Now that you know Micky Rudd, will you show him my new creation?" Chet begged.

"Well, uh—I'm not sure we'll have a chance," Frank stalled, "but if we do, we'll show it to him."

The Hardys were saved from making further

awkward excuses by the telephone ringing. The caller proved to be Buzz Barton.

"We're in business!" he reported excitedly. "I told the culties I wanted to be a Child of Noah, and they accepted me right off. There's a motor launch due in about half an hour to take a group out to the *Ark*, and I'm going with 'em!"

"Where's it anchored?" Frank asked.

"Just off Barmet Bay."

"Great! And do you have that special ladder we gave you?"

"Sure do! I pretended I've been on the road, so I'm carrying a small bedroll. The ladder's coiled up inside it. I also packed a flashlight, like you said."

Frank instructed Buzz on a set of signals and promised that he and Joe would bring their boat within sight of the *Ark* at 11:00 P.M.

About 10:15 P.M. the two youths drove to the boathouse where they stored their speedy craft, the *Sleuth*. Soon the sleek motorboat was planing out across the moonlit waters of Barmet Bay.

Presently the lights of the big, converted cruise liner became visible in the distance. It was anchored a mile or so north of the entrance to the bay.

Joe cut the engine and dropped the anchor. The Hardys transferred to a small plastic rowboat.

Dipping their oars gently, they rowed toward the *Ark*. It was a few minutes to eleven. As they approached the liner, two short flashes and one long flash of light shone from the ship.

"That means he's found Sue and she's ready to come with him!" Frank exclaimed in a whisper.

Rowing in closer, they found the special detective's climbing rig dangling over the side as arranged. It consisted of a slender nylon cable with plastic projections at intervals to serve as foot- and handholds.

Making their boat fast to the cable, the Hardys clambered up the ladder. But as they scrambled aboard the *Ark*, rough hands grabbed them in the darkness!

# 9

## Deep-Sixed!

Deck lights suddenly flashed on, including a spotlight aimed directly at the Hardy boys' eyes. They blinked and squinted in the dazzling glare and tried to avert their faces, but the hands gripping them tightly from behind prevented them from doing so.

Presently they were able to make out a man in captain's uniform. Another man, wearing third mate's stripes, was with him, as well as several shaven-headed, white-robed cultie youths.

"What's the big idea, grabbing us as if we were criminals!" Frank said boldly to the captain.

"What do you expect us to do when two harbor rats come sneaking aboard in the middle of the night?" the captain retorted roughly. "Shake hands and offer you a cup of coffee?"

"We came here to see a friend," put in Joe.

"Funny way to visit a friend, crawling aboard in the dark like a couple of sneak thieves!"

"We saw flashes of light from the deck, so we figured there must be someone on watch who could tell us if it was okay."

Joe would have liked to add sarcastically, "How do you suppose we could have climbed aboard if our friend hadn't put a ladder over the side for us?" But he realized that any such remark was only apt to cause worse trouble for Buzz Barton, if he was not already in an unpleasant predicament. In any case, their captors must be well aware of how they had clambered up the side.

"You were right about one thing!" the captain growled. "There *was* someone on watch! And now that you've been caught trespassing on my ship, you're going to be taught a lesson you won't forget! Give 'em the deep six, fellows!"

With hoots and cries the others closed in on the Hardys as the captain watched mockingly. Frank and Joe put up a fierce resistance, but they were overpowered by sheer numbers. The boys felt themselves picked up by a dozen hands. Next moment they were heaved over the side like jettisoned cargo!

*Kersplash!* They hit the water almost simultaneously. Breathless from their steep plunge and the shock of immersion in the cold water, the Hardys floundered wildly for a few moments.

Luckily both were good swimmers. They made it safely to their boat with three or four strong strokes. Boarding it without capsizing the craft was their next problem, but at last, soaked and panting, they flopped miserably into their little plastic rowboat.

Jeering laughter rang out from the deck of the liner above them. Then, with a noisy clatter, the nylon climbing rig was tossed down on top of them.

"Those cowards!" Joe raged, clenching his fists. "If only we could take 'em on two at a time!"

"Forget it," Frank said, gritting his teeth. "We did sneak aboard in the dark, and we knew we were taking a chance, so what's the use of blowing our tops?"

As they rowed back to the *Sleuth*, he added, "What worries me is what's going to happen to Buzz Barton!"

Joe shot an anxious glance at his brother. "You think they might really work him over?"

"Who knows? If that skipper's ruthless enough to throw us overboard, there's no telling what he and those Noah nuts might do to someone who joined the cult under false pretenses!"

"That's assuming they know Buzz is our friend and why he joined up."

"They're just bound to know!" Frank declared. "How else could they have gotten all set for us if they hadn't dredged the truth out of Buzz?"

"H'm!" Joe said worriedly. "Then maybe we ought to call Dad and ask him to do something to get Buzz out of this mess! We're the ones who got him into it!"

"Good idea! Let's try the radio!"

As soon as they got back to their motorboat, the boys warmed up the *Sleuth*'s powerful transceiver and beamed out the Hardys' emergency-code call. By luck, their broadcast brought an almost immediate response from their father, who happened to see the flashing signal on his own set that indicated an urgent transmission. "What's up, Sons?"

Frank hastily briefed him. The boys could tell from Fenton Hardy's tone of voice that he was as disturbed as they were over the situation.

"Go to the Coast Guard station as fast as possible and ask for help!" the famous manhunter advised. "Meantime, I'll call Washington!"

"Okay, Dad!"

Joe gunned the engine, and in seconds the *Sleuth* was carving a double bow wave of water as it sped toward the Barmet Bay Coast Guard station.

Much to their relief, a lieutenant was waiting to

receive them, and a launch was already warmed up and ready to shove off. "Your dad must have called some important people," the officer told the Hardy boys. "We've had an urgent request from the FBI as well as official authorization from our own department!"

The launch cruised swiftly across the bay and soon had the *Ark* pinned squarely in the glare of its powerful searchlights. As they pulled alongside the converted cruise liner, the lieutenant called out through an electric bullhorn:

"Prepare to receive a boarding party!"

Frank and Joe were allowed to accompany him. Both boys enjoyed the dismayed, trapped expression on the captain's face as the Coast Guard lieutenant barked, "You realize you could be hauled up before a board of inquiry and perhaps have your license suspended for what you did to these boys tonight?"

"They had no business trespassing on my ship!" the captain blustered.

"Don't give me that bilge!" the officer snapped. "This is the twentieth century! We're not living back in the days of keelhauling, and you're not Captain Bligh! Now then, we're here because fears have been expressed about the safety of a young man named Buzz Barton. We'd like to see him, please."

81

A white-robed man with a shaved head, who seemed somewhat older than most of the culties, spoke up. "We Children of Noah don't allow our brothers and sisters to be harassed by anyone, including the United States Coast Guard!"

The lieutenant stared at him coldly. "Nobody's interested in what you allow, mister, and we're not here to harass anybody. Well, Captain?"

"Do you have a search warrant?"

"No, because I'm not searching for anyone. I'm asking to speak to one of your passengers. And I might add that I'm doing so at the urgent request of the FBI. Now, do you want to cooperate or don't you?"

The captain hemmed and hawed and continued to bluster, but he was clearly uneasy over the Coast Guard's unexpected intervention.

In the end, he conducted the lieutenant and the Hardy boys to a cabin below deck, where Buzz Barton lay asleep on the bunk. When awakened, he seemed somewhat vague and confused, but there was no sign that he had been physically harmed.

"Are you aboard of your own free will?" the lieutenant asked.

"Y-Y-Yes, sir."

"Do you wish to remain aboard, or would you rather go back ashore with your friends?"

Buzz hesitated, blinking. Frank and Joe were unable to read the expression in his eyes. "I prefer to stay aboard," he mumbled at last.

The Noah cultie who had protested earlier now beamed triumphantly at the Hardys and the Coast Guard officer. Since there seemed to be no further reason to intervene, the boarding party returned to their launch.

Glumly the Hardy boys arrived at the Coast Guard station and cruised back to the Bayport marina in the *Sleuth*.

After breakfast the next morning, Frank called Vern Kelso, the network executive at the Federated Broadcasting System whom Micky Rudd had mentioned. "We're investigating that vandal who's impersonating the Apeman," Frank explained. "I wonder if you could spare time, sir, to talk to my brother and me?"

"You bet I can! We'll all be grateful for anything you fellows can do to find this pest and expose him." Kelso said that Micky Rudd had already told him about calling in the Hardy boys, and added, "How about having lunch with me today? Say one o'clock?"

"We'd like that! Thanks very much, Mr. Kelso. We'll be there."

The Hardys phoned Chet to tell him to get ready to come with them. Half an hour later as they were going out the door, the telephone rang.

Aunt Gertrude answered and called out, "Your father's on the line!"

"What's up, Dad?" Joe asked, taking the phone.

"My operatives have checked out those eight muscle men, son. Six of them have alibis, but two don't, and neither does Zack Amboy himself."

# 10

## An Urgent Message

Joe checked off the names of the suspects who had
no alibis for the times when the Apeman impostor
had carried out his malicious raids.

"Thanks, Dad! We'll follow up on those two and
Zack Amboy."

"Right. And remember my warning, Son," Fenton Hardy added, "about keeping your guard up."

"We won't forget, Dad," Joe promised.

Hanging up, he relayed the news to his brother.
Frank was interested to hear that Zack himself had
no alibi. "He also has no alibi for the time you got
conked outside the Olympic Gym," the older Hardy boy pointed out.

"But that phone call was no fake," Joe countered.

"I mean, even though no one spoke when you answered, I take it there *was* someone on the other end of the line, right?"

"Sure, but that's no problem. All he'd have had to do would be to call a friend and ask him to dial the gym office number and keep the line open for a few minutes. Zack could easily have done that fast enough to chase after us and say there was a call for me. Then he gabbed with you for a bit and pretended to leave but actually sneaked back and slugged you when you weren't looking."

Joe nodded thoughtfully. "Could be. But Zack sure didn't look like that kind of trickster!"

The Hardys drove out to the Morton farm to pick up Chet. Their stout chum had finished inking and coloring his Captain Muscles cartoons and was eager to show off his new hero at Star Comix.

"How much do you think they'll offer me if they decide to publish my story?" Chet asked eagerly.

"Maybe two bits, if you're lucky," Joe said but couldn't keep a straight face.

"Okay, wise guy!" Chet flared. "Just wait'll it turns out to be a big hit! You'll be begging for my autograph!"

Frank grinned but kept silent as they headed for the turnpike, which would take them to New York.

One of the strong-man suspects was a bank guard named Olafsen, who lived and worked in a small town that lay directly on their route. The boys turned off at the nearest exit and, after asking directions, found the bank on Main Street and parked in the customers' lot.

Inside, they had no trouble finding the right man. Two guards were standing near opposite doors. One was a paunchy, middle-aged type who looked as if he might be a retired policeman. The other was a tall, blond young man with a huge muscular chest and shoulders that strained the buttons of his uniform. Frank and Joe went up to him and introduced themselves.

"Mr. Olafsen, we've been asked to investigate the vandal who's been impersonating the Apeman," Frank said. "Probably you've heard about him in the news."

"Sure, but what's that got to do with me?" Olafsen responded coldly.

"Part of the investigation involves checking up on all expert body builders in this part of the country who might be big enough and strong enough to fill the bill."

"Look, fella! If you're trying to hang that rap on me, you've got another thing coming!"

"Nobody's trying to hang anything on you," Joe said. "Actually we want to *clear* everyone who's innocent. So if you've got nothing to hide, what's wrong with answering a few questions?"

87

"I've already answered a few questions, buddy," Olafsen grumbled. "Some private eye called me up last night and then barged around in person, asking me a lot of questions about where I was at such and such a time and a lot more baloney. Well, from now on I've got nothing more to say. What I do in my spare time is my own business and if you don't like it, tell the DA!"

The Hardy boys exchanged a few more remarks with the blond strong man. Their polite manner seemed to mollify him somewhat, but he remained unhelpful.

"What do you make of him, Frank?" Joe asked in a puzzled voice as they left the bank. "Think Olafsen could be the vandal?"

The older boy shrugged. "Maybe. He sure wasn't going out of his way to clear himself of suspicion. But let's not jump to any conclusions. Whatever Dad's operative said to him last night, something tells me he must've rubbed Olafsen the wrong way."

"That's for sure."

After parking their car in New York, Frank and Joe took Chet to the offices of Star Comix in Rockefeller Center and introduced him to Micky Rudd. Then they excused themselves and left to keep their luncheon appointment with Vern Kelso.

The headquarters and studios of the FBS network were located in a towering glass and steel skyscraper on the Avenue of the Americas. An express elevator whisked the Hardy boys to the executive suite on the twenty-fifth floor, where Kelso's attractive secretary greeted them and ushered them into his private office.

"So you're those famous young sleuths!" he said, jumping up to shake hands. "Can't tell you how delighted I am that you two are handling this case. Just bear with me, please, while I sign a few letters, and then we'll be off to lunch!"

Vern Kelso was a slim, expensively dressed man in his thirties, with curly brown hair and long sideburns. As he swiftly jotted his signature on a stack of letters, he kept up a brisk flow of conversation.

"Usually I have my car brought around to take me to lunch," he remarked. "Saves time flagging a taxi. But I didn't bother today."

"Our car's parked not far from here; we can take that, if you like," Frank offered.

"No, no, thanks all the same. I just live over on Sutton Place, near the UN, so there'd be no problem getting my own car. But my houseman, who also acts as chauffeur, isn't feeling well, and besides, it's such a nice day, I thought we might enjoy walking, if you don't mind."

"Fine with us." Joe grinned.

The Hardys would, indeed, have enjoyed the

stroll to the restaurant several blocks from the network building. But as they made their way in the bright sunshine through throngs of tourists and New Yorkers, the boys had the disturbing feeling that they were being shadowed again.

From their exchange of guarded glances, each guessed that the other was troubled by the same instinct. But despite their attempts to keep watch by means of shop-window reflections or cautious peeks over their shoulder, they could discover no one who seemed to be dogging their footsteps.

Kelso's secretary had reserved a table for them at the restaurant, which was crowded with gaily chattering, smartly dressed lunchers. The network executive explained that the place was patronized mostly by people in the television and fashion industries.

Privately Frank and Joe thought they could pick out the latter individuals by the far-out styles in which many of them were dressed.

Kelso regaled the boys with an entertaining if somewhat boastful account of how hard he had worked to sell "The Apeman" show to the Federated Broadcasting System.

"There's a lot of jealousy in this business," he confided. "Sometimes it seems as if everybody has his knife in someone else's back. I really stuck my neck out to get 'The Apeman' accepted. If the show had flopped, a lot of people at the network would have enjoyed seeing me take the blame. But it turned into a big hit, so now I'm having the last laugh!"

Kelso did not seem greatly worried over the unpleasant publicity caused by the vandal who had been impersonating the Apeman. Both Hardys had a sneaking hunch that he secretly enjoyed the publicity and felt that it attracted more viewers to the show.

Frank mentioned the list of suspects they had gotten from Zack Amboy and added, "Is there any chance some television actor might be doing the impersonating? Maybe someone who hoped to get the Apeman role himself, and then got sore because he lost out?"

Vern Kelso shook his head emphatically. "No way. Micky Rudd and I had our eye on Dante Mazzola right from the start, and he's the muscle man we finally picked. There was never any real competition for the part."

The conversation was interrupted as a waiter brought a plug-in telephone to their table.

"Call from the network, Mr. Kelso!"

"Thanks." Kelso picked up the receiver and answered, then glanced at the Hardy boys. "It's for you two, a call from home. My secretary's having it relayed here."

He held out the handset toward Frank, who took it somewhat worriedly. "Hello?"

"G here," said a sharp voice at the other end of the line. "You've just had a message from SR. He's in New York and wants to see you right away. He says it's urgent!"

# *11*

## *Another Amulet*

Frank pulled out pencil and paper and hastily wrote down directions.

"Thanks, Aunt Gertrude. We'll go see him as soon as possible," he said and hung up.

Turning to his brother, Frank said, "Something's come up, apparently urgent. Sam Radley wants to see us."

Sam was Fenton Hardy's top operative and had often worked with the Hardy boys on previous cases.

Finishing their dessert hastily, the boys apologized to Vern Kelso for the untimely interruption, and after thanking him for the lunch, left the restaurant.

"Any idea what's up?" Joe asked as he and Frank headed east on foot.

"Not a clue. But I do know Sam's been working on that stolen art-goods case for Dad."

In the case Frank was referring to, Mr. Hardy had been hired by an insurance company to help break up a traffic in stolen paintings and other art objects.

They found Sam Radley waiting unobtrusively in a doorway on East Fifty-ninth Street. The detective was on stakeout, keeping watch on the shop of a shady art dealer across the street.

"Sorry it took us so long to get here, Sam," Frank apologized. "We figured walking would be quicker than trying to buck the crosstown traffic in a cab."

"No sweat," Sam replied. "Actually, you made it sooner than I expected. Your aunt must have gotten in touch with you right away."

As the boys already knew, their father made it a practice to circulate pictures of any suspects or wanted persons among whatever operatives were working for him at the time. One such person was Paul Linwood's missing daughter, Sue.

"I just spotted her," Sam reported, "a few minutes before I phoned your home in Bayport."

The Hardys were startled. Did this mean that the girl they were trying to find had *not* joined the Children of Noah cult?

94

"Are you sure it was Sue Linwood you saw, Sam?" Joe asked.

"Positive—or else it was her double. She delivered a package to that art dealer's shop. Then she left in a taxi. Luckily I got the number."

"Great! Let me have it and I'll check it out."

"You won't have to. I've already done that." Radley explained that, while waiting for the Hardy boys to arrive from the restaurant, he had called the New York Police Department from a telephone booth down the street and had gotten a quick trace of the cab's owner-driver over the police computer system. "There's his name and address."

Frank grinned as he took the slip of paper from the operative. "Sam, you're terrific!"

In the lobby of a nearby office building, the Hardys found directories for the various New York City boroughs and got the phone number of the driver, who lived in Brooklyn. His wife answered Frank's call.

"Vinnie isn't here," she replied. "He's working days now. Try him after seven."

"This is fairly urgent, ma'am. Is there any way we could reach him?"

"Well, let's see. It's about a quarter after two. He usually eats between one and two, but sometimes if he's real busy, he won't have lunch till later. You might try the diner where he always goes. The counterman could tell you if Vinnie's been in yet." She gave Frank the location of the diner on the Lower East Side of Manhattan.

"Thanks a lot, ma'am! We'll give it a try."

The boys hailed a taxi and were driven to the diner. Its noontime rush of business was over, and only a single customer was seated at the counter, a chunky, dark-haired man in a red sport shirt and checkered slacks.

The proprietor asked the boys, "May I help you?"

When Frank inquired about the cab driver by name, he jerked a thumb toward the dark-haired man in the red shirt and grinned. "You're looking at him."

"What a break!" Joe exclaimed. He and Frank promptly introduced themselves to Vinnie, who turned out to know all about the famous young sleuths. In fact, he had seen their recent interview on television.

"No kiddin'! Are you two really the Hardy boys?" he blurted as they shook hands. "Well, I'll be! Come on, sit down and have a milkshake or something."

When Frank explained why they had come, Vinnie was eager to help. "Sure, I know the fare you're talking about. Real pretty girl, about eighteen. I took her up on the East Side and picked up another fare downtown, and that's when I knocked off for lunch."

"Do you remember the address you took her to?" Frank asked.

"No address. There was a car waiting for her. I saw her get into it as I drove off."

"What kind of a car?"

"A red Mercedes sedan. But if you wanna know the license number, you're outa luck. I didn't even notice what..." The chunky, dark-haired cab driver broke off suddenly and stuck his hand into his shirt pocket. "Hey, wait a second. Here's something that might interest you if you're trying to trace her. I almost forgot about it."

He held out an amulet. On one side was an image of a flying bird with an olive branch in its mouth, exactly like the design on the amulet found at the park disco!

"I'll say this interests us!" Frank exclaimed. "Where'd it come from?"

"The fare I picked up in the next block noticed it as he got into my hack. I figured it mighta fallen out when the girl opened her purse to pay me."

"Can we hang onto this for the time being? I'll give you a receipt for it, if you like."

"Naw, don't bother. Just keep it and give it to her when you find her, with my compliments."

"Thanks! We'll do that, Vinnie. You've helped us a lot!"

"My pleasure. Listen, my son Dino'll really be

excited when I tell him I helped the Hardy boys on one of their mystery cases!"

Frank and Joe grinned and shook hands with the cabby, then left the diner.

"If this amulet means anything," Frank mused, "it looks like Mr. Linwood's hunch was right after all, I mean, about Sue joining the Children of Noah."

"Sure does," Joe agreed. "But if she has, then what's she doing delivering a package to a crooked art dealer?"

"Search me. I think we ought to call Dad about this."

Mr. Hardy answered on the first ring when Frank dialed his number from a nearby phone booth. He was keenly interested to hear about the red Mercedes sedan that had picked up Sue Linwood.

"The head of the Children of Noah is a fellow called Noah Norvel," the ace detective remarked. "He's been in the news a good deal lately, on charges of brainwashing his young cult members and preventing them from seeing their parents. So the FBI has had their eye on him. He has a huge estate in Westchester County just north of New York City, where he keeps a whole fleet of personal cars. If I'm not mistaken, one of them is a red Mercedes."

"If you're right, that may be another clue indicating Sue has joined his cult," said Frank. "Do you think there's any chance she may be staying at his estate, Dad—I mean, assuming the red car does belong to Noah?"

"I think it's definitely worth checking out." Fenton Hardy gave the boys directions for reaching Noah's estate.

Frank and Joe contacted Chet Morton over a pocket walkie-talkie, as arranged beforehand, and met their chum fifteen minutes later at the parking garage where they had left their car. As the Bayport trio drove up through the Bronx on their way out of the city, Chet proudly informed the Hardys that Micky Rudd had kept his cartoons so they could be looked over by other members of the Star Comix staff.

"Nice going, Chet!" Joe congratulated their pal. "We may now be traveling with a future famous cartoonist!"

In the hope of picking up a possible clue in the case of the fake Apeman, the Hardys decided to stop at the home of the late artist, Archie Frome. Hamp Huber had given them Frome's address in a suburb overlooking Long Island Sound.

It turned out that Frome had been a widower. His married daughter, a pleasant young woman named Mrs. Elver, was busy cleaning the house. She invited the boys to come in and sit down while she answered their questions but kept a tight grip on the collar of an enormous Irish wolfhound that pranced and growled eagerly at the sight of the visitors.

"Don't be afraid of Rory." She smiled. "He's like a big puppy. The trouble is, he's apt to knock you down, trying to make you feel at home."

Aside from a sofa and two chairs, the living room looked somewhat bare.

"I've already been through Dad's studio and donated a lot of his drawings and paintings to the Comic Art Museum," Mrs. Elver said. "Now I'm disposing of most of the furniture."

"What's the Comic Art Museum?" Chet asked.

The cartoonist's daughter said that many of the people involved in producing cartoon strips and comic books had purchased a building in a nearby town in Westchester and turned it into a museum for storing and displaying the artwork in their field.

"Oh, I'd like to see that place!" Chet exclaimed. Mrs. Elver told the boys its location.

Frank explained why they had come, then asked, "Do you have any idea why your father might have called Micky Rudd 'a real crook'?"

The young woman shook her head. "I've been married for over seven years now, so I was sort of out of touch with Dad's work. I do know he got fed up with the comic book business, so these last few years he spent all his time illustrating children's books."

Mrs. Elver frowned thoughtfully and added, "However, I do remember Dad mentioning there was a mysterious burglary here."

# 12

## A Ghostly Figure

The Hardy boys' detective instinct was immediately stirred upon hearing of the burglary.

"What was taken?" Joe asked.

"Nothing, that's the odd part about it. Yet there were valuables in plain sight, like an expensive camera and a new TV and a video cassette recorder in the living room, not to mention all the silverware in the dining room, or a cut-glass punchbowl that's worth several hundred dollars. But the robber passed it all up!"

"How did you find out about the burglary?" Frank inquired.

"Dad told me about it. It happened shortly before he died."

"No, ma'am, I mean how did *he* find out there

had been a burglary if nothing was taken?"

"Oh, because Rory chased the robber away. He'd been snoozing alongside Dad's bed, the way he always did, but I guess he finally heard some noises and woke up and went galumphing downstairs to see what was going on. Then his growls and the commotion woke Dad. Apparently the robber just had time to make it out the front door before Rory took off an arm or a leg."

"Maybe the thief had no time to steal anything," Joe suggested.

Mrs. Elver looked doubtful. "I don't know. Dad said there were signs that he must've been searching the downstairs rooms quite thoroughly before Rory got after him. There was even Dad's gold wristwatch lying out in plain view on the drawing board in his studio. The thief could have slipped that in his pocket, but he didn't."

The Hardys could offer no solution to the mysterious burglary. But they promised to let Mrs. Elver know if it proved to have any connection with the Apeman case.

When the boys returned to their car, Joe studied a road map briefly. "Look," he pointed out, "the place where that other muscle-man suspect works is about ten miles from here. Why don't we detour there and talk to him?"

"Suits me," said Frank, and Chet made no objection.

The man in question was a mechanic named Vic Cardiff. He was employed at a highway gas station and proved to be a sullen-looking, belligerent type with beetling black brows and a heavy jaw.

"I know all about you guys," Cardiff said, brushing aside Frank's attempted introduction. "You're those two punks who think they're smart detectives just because their old man's a private eye. Right now you're mixed up with this nut who goes around posing as the Apeman and smashing things up."

"We're not mixed up with him," Joe said. "We're trying to find out who he is."

"And you think maybe I'm the guy, huh?"

"I didn't say that."

"It's what you meant, though," the muscular mechanic growled. "Why else would you be looking me up? Well, you're barking up the wrong tree, so beat it!"

"All we want to do is ask you a few questions," said Frank, standing his ground. "If you've got nothing to hide, what's wrong with talking to us?"

"You heard me! I've got nothing to say to you guys, so scram outa here! I got work to do." Without another word, Cardiff turned away and went back to greasing a car that was up on a hoist.

"Nice guy," Chet muttered as the boys climbed back into the Hardys' sporty car.

"Like they say, it takes all kinds," Frank said,

starting the vehicle and turning out into the stream of highway traffic.

"Yes, and it takes all kinds of clues to solve a mystery," Joe added wryly. "Only we didn't get any free ones from him!"

It was late afternoon when the Bayporters reached their destination. They had to ask directions at another gas station in order to find Noah's mansion. It was located several miles from the nearest town on a narrow wooded road that was little more than a country lane.

The imposing stone house was well screened from the road by trees. There was no wall or fence enclosing the grounds, but the boys glimpsed at least two armed guards on patrol as they drove past, and also a series of huge, white-painted boulders, which apparently marked the boundaries of the estate.

"Got any plan?" Joe asked his brother. "Or do we just walk up and ring the doorbell?"

Frank shook his head. "Not yet. That would only put Noah on guard, and we might not learn anything. I think our best bet is to keep watch on the place, say for twenty-four hours anyhow, and see if we can spot Sue Linwood going in or out."

After driving a little farther, Frank pulled off the road. The boys got out of the car and walked through the woods back toward Noah's mansion. Scouting around cautiously, they found a low-branched tree that afforded a clear view of the house and attached garage.

"That should do for a stakeout," Joe said, and his two companions agreed.

Only two cars were visible on the drive, neither of them a red Mercedes, but the Hardys realized there might be other cars behind the closed doors of the garage.

After checking in at a nearby motel and phoning their homes in Bayport, the three boys ate a hasty supper of hamburgers and french fries, then they drew straws to see who would stand the first lookout. Joe picked the shortest one, giving him the first watch from six to nine. Chet would get the next, from nine to midnight.

"If either of you sees anything interesting, give a buzz on the walkie-talkie," Frank instructed.

"Right," said Chet. "Better get some munchies to keep me awake." As they paid at the cashier's counter, the stout boy bought a bag of peanuts, some grape-flavored gum, and two candy bars.

"Just don't eat yourself to sleep," Joe warned.

Driving back to the wooded lane, Frank and Chet dropped off the younger Hardy boy near the stakeout tree, then returned to their motel, where Chet settled down for an early nap. At nine he relieved Joe, who had nothing to report.

Sometime later, Frank was roused by the buzzing of the walkie-talkie. He groped for the set sleepily and pressed the switch to communicate. "H-1 here."

"I just saw something spooky!" Chet's voice crackled over the speaker.

"Like what?"

"A *ghost*—that's what!"

"Are you kidding?"

"No, honest! There's a white figure moving around through the trees. I've caught sight of it twice!"

"Did you try to trail it or find out who it was?"

"N-Not yet." A faint gulp came over the walkie-talkie. Chet's voice quavered a bit, but he went on bravely, "If the figure shows up again, I'll try and grab it. But how about some backup?"

"We'll be right with you," Frank promised.

Joe was already awake. Frank relayed the news as they flung on their clothes. Then the Hardys hurried out to their car and sped toward the scene of action. Rather than risk any attention by driving past at such a late hour, they parked and skirted the mansion on foot.

But the lookout tree was empty!

Frank gave a soft owl-hoot signal. No one responded. A slightly louder hoot still drew no response. Worried, the Hardys searched about cautiously but could find no trace of their roly-poly chum. *Chet had disappeared!*

107

# 13

## The Face at the Window

Joe was inclined to plunge on boldly and search the grounds of Noah Norvel's mansion. But his brother stopped him with a hand on his arm.

"Take it easy," Frank advised. "We could be walking right into a trap!"

"We've got to find Chet, haven't we?" Joe retorted.

"Sure, but he may already have been lured into a trap. It won't help him much if we fall for the same trick."

"How do you mean?"

Frank pointed to two nearby white boundary stones. "Those boulders mark the edge of Noah's estate. I've got a hunch that white spook was just bait to draw Chet over the line."

Joe frowned uneasily. "You mean one of the

108

guards may have spotted Chet in the tree?"

"Right. So he passes the word, and another one puts on a white robe and starts flitting around among the trees, just enough to catch Chet's eye. Then when Chet tries to follow the ghost, they wait till he steps over the line and nab him. He's now trespassing on Noah's property, so that gives them the right to arrest him."

"Wow! You could be right, Frank. That would sure explain where Chet disappeared to. But what are we going to do about it?"

Frank puckered his forehead thoughtfully for a moment, then said, "I'm in favor of a direct approach, Joe. Let's go right up to the front door and find out what's what."

"Well, if you say so, I'll go along! What've we got to lose?"

The two boys hurried back to their car, which was parked on the shoulder among some trees, and drove out onto the road again. As they turned up the driveway of Noah's estate, a guard suddenly stepped out into view from among the shrubbery and held up his hand to signal them to stop.

As Frank braked to a halt, the guard challenged them roughly. "What do you guys want here? Don't you know Mr. Norvel doesn't receive visitors this late at night?"

Frank acted on a sudden hunch. Instead of replying, he pulled out the amulet that the taxi

109

driver had given him and showed it to the guard.

The sight of the metal token bearing the dove and olive-branch symbol seemed to take the guard by surprise. He stared at it for a moment with a puzzled scowl, then at the two boys. Finally he muttered, "Okay," and waved them on.

"Smart move, Frank!" Joe chuckled as their car continued up the driveway. "Looks like those amulets must be used as identification by the cultists, eh?"

"Right, at least by the ones who have direct contact with Noah. It also means there must have been a Child of Noah at the Alfresco Disco the other night, when the fake Apeman raided the costume party." Frank broke off as he glanced in the rearview mirrow. "Uh, oh!"

"What's the matter?" his brother asked.

"The guard's calling someone on his walkie-talkie. Something tells me we're about to be met by a welcoming committee!"

As their car drew up at the top of the drive and the Hardys got out, Joe suddenly gasped. Frank saw that he was staring at one of the upper-story windows of the mansion.

"See something?" the elder Hardy boy asked.

"Some*one*!" Joe corrected. "See that window-with the fringe of light? A girl up there was closing the Venetian blind just now, but I got a quick look at her face. I think she was Sue Linwood!"

110

"Could you swear to that, if we have to call the police about Chet?"

Joe hesitated unhappily. "No, I'm not absolutely certain," he admitted. "But she sure looked like the girl in the picture Mr. Linwood gave us, and *he* thinks she joined Noah's cult. I'd say that adds up to pretty fair circumstantial evidence, or at least grounds for suspicion."

"So would I," Frank agreed. "Let's see how far it'll get us."

The Hardys walked boldly up to the entrance of the mansion. But before they could ring the bell, the front door suddenly opened. A youthful, shaven-headed cult member in a white robe stared out at them suspiciously.

"Peace be with you, brothers," he mumbled in a voice that was noticeably lacking in brotherly warmth.

Frank introduced himself and Joe, adding, "We'd like to see Mr. Noah Norvel."

Instead of answering, the white-robed cultie stepped aside, and a tall, heavyset man appeared in the doorway. His skin was deeply tanned to a walnut brown, and his long blond hair and bushy beard were sun-bleached almost white. He was clad in a gold satin jumpsuit.

"You are seeing Noah now," the man announced with a mocking smile. "I've been expecting you Hardys. Come in!"

111

He moved backward and waved them inside with a gesture that also seemed somehow mocking.

As the Hardys entered, they saw the reason for his sarcastic amusement. Their pal, Chet Morton, was lying face down on the floor with his wrists handcuffed behind his back! The fat boy's face was flushed with embarrassment and the discomfort caused by his awkward position.

"What's the big idea?" Joe blurted indignantly at the cult leader. "He's a friend of ours!"

"Indeed?" Noah responded with a malicious twinkle. "Then perhaps you can explain what he was doing spying on my house and trespassing on my property?"

Frank spoke up quickly, "Did you ask him?"

"Of course! And the only answer he could give me was some cock-and-bull story about chasing a ghost. Can you imagine?"

"Sure, I can imagine. Your followers wear white robes, don't they? Maybe Chet saw one of them in the darkness and thought it was a ghost. Whatever he saw, or thought he saw, that doesn't give you any right to handcuff him and treat him like a criminal!"

Noah's voice and expression hardened. "On the contrary! I could call the police and file an official complaint against him! But I won't—providing you Hardys promise not to subject me to any more harassment."

"Nobody's harassing you," Frank said coldly.

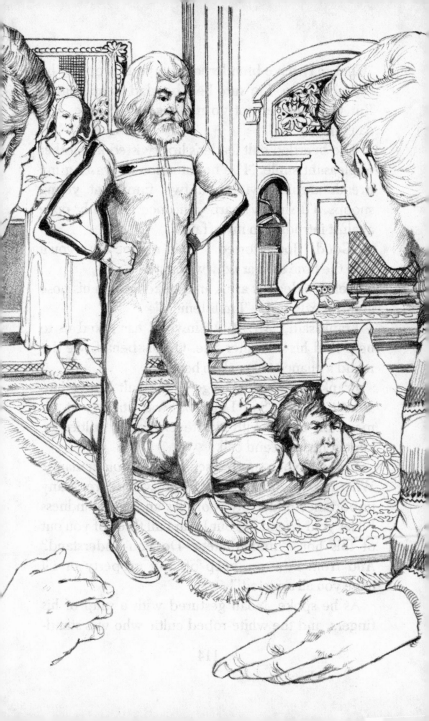

"Chet may have blundered onto your property by mistake. If so, I'm sure he'll be glad to apologize. But you'd better not go making any charges you can't prove."

The bearded cult leader's lips twisted in another unpleasant smile. "I've no intention of wasting my breath arguing with you two impudent young snoops. I'll simply warn you once and only once against intruding in my affairs."

"Good!" Joe retorted. "Then maybe now you'll take the time to hear why we came."

Noah folded his arms and looked down his nose at the Hardy boys. "I'm listening."

Frank said, "Mr. Paul Linwood has asked us to help find his daughter Sue. On his behalf, we demand a chance to speak to her."

Frank was hoping to goad the cult leader into admitting that Sue Linwood was staying at his mansion, along with whatever young culties he kept at his beck and call.

Instead, Noah snorted scornfully. "*You* demand? What makes you think that your wishes are of any importance under my roof? As an act of kindness I'll let your friend go, but I want all three of you out of this house immediately. Do you understand? And from now on, keep off my property or I'll have you all arrested!"

As he spoke, Noah gestured with a snap of his fingers, and the white-robed cultie who was standing by proceeded to remove the handcuffs from Chet's wrists. The plump youth got up sheepishly and left the mansion with the Hardys.

"That big phony!" Joe fumed as they climbed into the sleek yellow car.

"Guess I really messed things up," Chet confessed glumly. "I was trying to catch up with that ghost, and the first thing I knew, two guards jumped out from behind the trees and grabbed me!"

"Never mind, it wasn't your fault, Chet," said Frank. "You were deliberately set up, which means they must have spotted you up in the tree. Or maybe they spotted all of us earlier on."

Back at their motel, the three Bayporters were about to turn in for the night when the telephone rang. Chet answered, then held out the phone to Joe, who was nearer to him. "For you Hardys. It's your Aunt Gertrude."

Surprised and a bit alarmed, Joe took the handset and said, "Hi, Aunty! Everything okay at home?"

"Yes, indeed, your mother and I have everything under control! But have you heard the latest news bulletin?"

"No. What's up?"

"That scoundrel who's impersonating the Ape-man has gone on another rampage!" Miss Hardy informed her nephew.

Joe gasped. "Whereabouts, Aunty?"

"At a place called the Comic Art Museum!"

# 14

## Stolen Secrets

Joe was more startled than ever to hear that the museum which the Hardy boys had just heard about for the first time that afternoon should be the scene of the weird vandal's latest raid.

After asking a few more questions, he said, "Thanks for the tip, Aunt Gertrude. This may be important!"

"Indeed it is!" Miss Hardy snapped. "If I hadn't thought so, I wouldn't have called at this late hour. Mark my words, there were probably drawings of the Apeman at the museum, and the culprit went there to destroy them as part of a revenge plot against the Apeman and everything connected with him. My theory is the culprit's gone loony, maybe from reading too many comic books!"

"You could be right at that, Aunty," Joe said, smothering a chuckle. Hanging up, he relayed the news to his two companions.

Frank was keenly interested and wide awake on hearing of this development. "I sure wish we could get a look at the scene of the break-in," he fretted. "We might turn up a really important clue!"

"We can stop off at the place tomorrow," Chet said sleepily. He had just finished peeling off his jeans and was settling himself comfortably in bed.

"By that time they may have the damage all tidied up," said Frank, "and the clues will be gone." He glanced at his watch, then added, "It's not much after ten-thirty. I wonder if the police would still be at the museum? There wouldn't be much traffic on the road at this time of night. I bet we could drive there in half an hour!"

"We could try calling the museum and see if anyone answers," Joe suggested.

"Good idea!" Frank strode to the phone and got an outside line, then dialed information and asked for the number of the Comic Art Museum.

"Do you want the regular number or the after-hours number?" the operator inquired.

"The after-hours number, if there's one listed."

"Yes, there is." She read it out.

Frank tried the number and circled a thumb and forefinger at Joe when his ringing got a prompt response. The answering voice turned out to be that of the museum director, a Mr. Gerald Tappan. He sounded gratified at the Hardy boys' interest in the night's mysterious event and invited the famous young sleuths to come as soon as possible to look for clues.

Chet preferred to stay settled for the night, but Frank and Joe started out immediately and reached their destination by eleven-twenty.

The museum was located in a small converted factory building. The director and his wife lived in the former owner's house just across the road. Tappan, who they learned was himself a cartoonist, greeted the Hardys cordially and unlocked the museum for their inspection.

"How did you happen to discover the break-in?" Joe asked him.

"Well, in summertime, you see, the museum is open till nine every weekday evening," Tappan replied. "Tonight, soon after I closed up, my wife noticed a glimmer of light over here, as if someone might be shining a flashlight inside. Next thing we knew, there were noises, loud enough to be heard clear across the road. So I went over to see what was going on."

"Isn't there any alarm system?" Frank put in.

"Not yet. The museum just exists on donations, and so far we haven't been able to afford one. Besides, this is a nice quiet area with a low crime rate.

I thought perhaps some youngster had just broken in for a prank."

Instead, Tappan related, he had discovered the brutal figure of the Apeman, or the Apeman impostor, tearing down drawings from the walls and wrecking exhibits.

"Did he try to attack you?" Joe asked.

"You bet he did!" Tappan replied ruefully. "He snatched up a bench and looked as if he were ready to break it over my head! I ran back out the door and across the road to my house and phoned the police. Unfortunately, the nut was gone by the time they arrived."

The vandalism was evident in the smears defacing the walls, drawings scattered about the floor, and several three-dimensional exhibits, such as a collection of toys based on comic strip characters, smashed as if with a fist or stick.

"I haven't even assessed the total damages yet," Tappan concluded. "Frankly, I was so upset that when the police and a local reporter finished looking over the situation, I just locked up and went home."

"Did the police find out how the guy got in?"

"Yes, through a rear window."

A broken pane and damage to the frame and sill indicated that the window had been levered open by the intruder.

As Frank stood eyeing the broken window, a sudden thought flashed through his head. "Have you received some work by an artist who's now dead, named Archie Frome?" he asked the museum director.

Tappan looked puzzled at the question. "Why, yes. It arrived just a couple of days ago, a whole crateful of his work. I haven't even had time to unpack it and go through it yet. Why?"

"Is it still here?"

Tappan's expression changed from puzzled to startled. "I—I don't know. I'll go see!"

He led the way to a storage room behind the museum office and went directly to a large crate. To his obvious dismay, the top of the crate had been pried off and the contents looked somewhat disordered, as though someone might have gone through them.

"Good night!" Tappan exclaimed. "How did you know?"

"Just a shot in the dark," said Frank. "Is there any way of telling what's been taken?"

"I'm not sure. Let me see."

As the museum director examined the contents of the crate, it soon became obvious that the drawings and other artwork were arranged in large file folders, with each folder labeled according to the year in which the work had been done.

"One whole year's work is missing!" Tappan exclaimed.

"What date?" Frank asked.

"Six years ago."

The Hardys were thoughtful as they thanked the museum director and started back to the motel in their car a short time later.

"Boy, what a weird case!" Joe remarked with a frown as they sped along the moonlit highway. "Do you suppose that artwork in the crate was the real motive for the break-in?"

"I'd be willing to bet on it," Frank said. "Whatever was in that missing folder may have been the same thing the thief who tried to rob Frome's house was after. That time he was out of luck because Frome's big wolfhound scared him off. But this time he found what he was looking for."

"So the damage to the museum exhibits was just a cover-up to mislead the cops!"

"Maybe, but we can't be sure of that, Joe. Remember, the faker who's posing as the Apeman has vandalized other places, too, where there was no artwork involved, like that movie theater in Shoreham and the disco at Bayport."

"True." Joe pinched his lower lip thoughtfully and continued frowning. "Speaking of the Alfresco Disco—do you suppose there's any connection between this case and the Noah cult? Or was it just a coincidence, the amulet turning up at the disco after the fake-Apeman raid?"

Frank shrugged and shook his head. "You've got me there."

121

"Hey, wait a minute!" Joe snapped his fingers excitedly. "I just remembered something."

"What?"

"Do you remember that TV news show a couple of months ago that told about the Children of Noah? It was a whole hour-long program on religious cults that seem to cause trouble between young people and their parents."

Frank flashed his brother a startled look. "Yes, I sure do, now that you mention it!"

"If I'm not mistaken, that program was broadcast by the FBS network, and it really gave the Children of Noah cult a rough going-over. Do you suppose Noah wants revenge, and this Apeman thing is his way of getting even?"

"You may be onto something there, Joe!"

Next day, after the Hardy boys and Chet returned to Bayport from the motel where they had stayed overnight, Frank telephoned Vern Kelso in New York to ask his opinion of Joe's theory.

"I'd say it's definitely possible," the television executive replied. For the first time, Kelso sounded worried. But he could offer no helpful leads by which to verify the theory.

"We'll try to check it out," Frank promised.

Next, the two boys tried to contact their father by telephone. His number got no answer, but after transmitting his code call repeatedly, they finally got a response over the radio.

"What's up, Son?" Fenton Hardy inquired.

"Dad, is there any connection between the stolen-art case that Sam Radley's working on and the Children of Noah cult?" Joe spoke into the mike.

There was a slight hesitation before Mr. Hardy's voice responded over the loudspeaker. "Yes, there is. Since this transmission is scrambled, I daresay I can answer your question briefly over the air, providing we don't go into details."

The famed detective explained that certain U.S. government security data, as well as stolen industrial trade secrets, were being sold to foreign agents overseas. The CIA had picked up various clues that seemed to point to Noah Norvel as the seller.

"I was hired to check him out," Mr. Hardy continued. "So far I've had no luck in getting the goods on him. But I did run across evidence indicating that Noah may be involved in another criminal racket, namely, the fencing of stolen jewelry and stolen paintings and other art objects." In every instance, the detective added, a fake or forgery had been substituted for the authentic stolen item.

"Then when Paul Linwood asked me to find his daughter," Mr. Hardy went on, "I hoped that might open up another line of investigation into Noah's criminal activities. But even that visit Sue paid to the shady art dealer, when Sam spotted her, doesn't really give us any conclusive proof."

Soon after Frank and Joe signed off their radio

conversation with their father, the telephone rang in the front hall. Frank answered and heard the voice of the Coast Guard lieutenant who had led the boarding party onto the *Ark*.

"We've just had a radio call from the *Ark*," he reported. "Apparently your friend Buzz Barton's had a bellyful of the Noah cult. He wants to be picked up. Can you go and get him?"

"Yes, sir, we'll leave right now! Thanks for letting us know."

The Hardy boys hurried out to their car and sped off to their boathouse near the harbor. But to their dismay after climbing aboard the *Sleuth*, the engine failed to respond when Joe keyed the ignition.

"Dead as a doornail!" he groaned.

"Hang on," said Frank. "Maybe just a loose connection somewhere."

Opening the engine compartment, he attempted to spot the cause. But the job of troubleshooting proved far more difficult than Frank had expected. Almost an hour of sweaty checking was performed by both boys before Frank exclaimed, "Here's the trouble, Joe—and it's no accident! Our starter relay has been sabotaged."

# 15

## Code-Word Clues

Joe was furious but also puzzled by their failure to notice any sign that the boathouse lock had been tampered with.

"That doesn't prove anything," Frank pointed out. "Any guy who's smart enough mechanically to pick a lock can easily make it shut again." He added a moment later, "Look—he didn't even leave any scratches!"

"But why worry about all that?" Joe asked. "If he's going to sabotage our boat, what difference does it make whether we know he broke in or not?"

"Just a nasty sense of humor, I guess. If we knew the boathouse had been broken into, we'd be prepared to find something wrong with the *Sleuth*.

This way, we don't discover the sabotage till we're all set to shove off."

"Great!" said Joe, looking disgusted. "So how're we going to pick up Buzz?"

"Maybe we can get Tony Prito to take us in his boat," Frank suggested.

"Great idea! Let's give him a call!"

The Hardys tried Tony's number from a nearby phone booth. Their high-school chum readily agreed to take them out to the *Ark* in his motorboat, the *Napoli*.

While they were sitting at the boat landing, waiting for Tony to appear, Frank remarked to Joe, "You know, there could be another reason why our boathouse was broken into."

"Such as?"

"The intruder might have been looking for something, maybe to see if we had any incriminating information in connection with one of the cases we're working on."

"We haven't used the *Sleuth* so far," said Joe, "in investigating the Apeman mystery."

"No, but we did the night we spotted those flashing-light signals from Buzz and went aboard the *Ark* to find Sue," Frank reminded his brother.

"That's right! So maybe the captain of the *Ark* or one of Noah's stooges got worried that we might be watching their ship, maybe snapping pictures of everyone who goes aboard."

"Right—or even just keeping a log of how many people come and go. Perhaps they hoped to find something in the boathouse that would tip them off to what we're up to, and sabotaging the *Sleuth* was just an afterthought."

"That would explain it, all right," Joe agreed.

Presently, Tony Prito's *Napoli* pulled alongside the boat landing. Frank and Joe clambered into the cockpit with him, and the trio were soon knifing out across the sunlit waters of Barmet Bay.

They could see a number of people, including white-robed culties, sailors, and at least one officer, watching them from the deck of the *Ark* as they approached the big converted cruise liner.

Frank cupped his hands and shouted up, "We've come for Buzz Barton!"

"Watch out, then!" the officer called back. "Here he comes!"

He turned and gestured to someone behind him with a wave of his hand. The Hardys and Tony saw a struggling figure being dragged toward the rail.

Next moment the prisoner was picked up bodily and hurled out over the side, hitting the water with a mighty splash not far from the *Napoli!*

Luckily the husky, freckle-faced youth seemed unharmed by his dunking. He swam toward the *Napoli* with brisk, powerful strokes, and the three Bayporters helped him scramble into the boat.

"What a bunch of yellow punks!" Tony exploded

angrily, glaring up at the grinning faces on the deck of the *Ark*.

"Don't waste your breath on 'em," Buzz Barton advised. "The poor saps aren't worth it."

On their way back to the harbor, Buzz related what had happened on the evening that he went aboard the cult ship. "They must've known beforehand that I was Sue Linwood's boyfriend and maybe that I was working with you Hardys, too," Buzz conjectured. "As soon as I went below, a couple of the culties grabbed me, and one of them jabbed me with a needle. After that, everything's a blur!"

"You were probably injected with something to make you talk," said Joe, "like a hypnotic drug. That's how they must have found out Frank and I were coming later and the signals to lure us aboard."

Buzz nodded. "That's what I thought. I didn't come to again till you fellows and that Coast Guard lieutenant woke me up in my bunk. By that time I figured the damage was done, so I might as well stay aboard and try to find out as much as I could."

"Any luck?" Frank inquired.

"Not much. Right now the only thing I'm pretty sure of is that Sue's not on the *Ark*."

"You're right, she isn't. As a matter of fact, she was seen yesterday in New York City." Frank explained how one of his father's operatives had spotted the missing girl and how he and Joe had tried to find out if she was staying at Noah's mansion.

Buzz in turn told how, after finding out all he could, he had persuaded the captain of the *Ark* to let him go. "I acted as mean and troublesome as possible," he chuckled, "picking fights with everyone and refusing to do any work. The skipper and the cultie in charge finally told me to scram and let me send a radio message to the Coast Guard!"

Barmet Bay was busy with fishing boats and other harbor traffic, including a huge oil tanker that was being nudged into its berth by a tug. As Tony slowed the *Napoli* and steered toward the boat landing, the Hardys quizzed Sue's boyfriend for further information on the cult.

Buzz reported that while the *Ark* hovered offshore, a whole fleet of smaller craft plied back and forth between the mother ship and various coastal ports, such as Bayport.

"In each town, there's an agent who drums up work for the culties," Buzz said. "You know, like painting or lawn work or jobs as temporary maids or houseboys. One thing I'll say for the Children of Noah, that cult teaches the kids to work hard and be very polite. And people soon find that out, so they're happy to be able to hire them."

"Which also makes a lot of money for the cult," Joe remarked.

"Right. The kids are told that it all goes into the cult treasury. But I'd be willing to bet that means Noah's private bank accounts!"

Buzz squinted out across the glittering sheet of spray furrowing aft from the bow. "I don't know if it means anything," he went on after a moment, "but I overheard a conversation on the *Ark* not long after you guys showed up."

"Who was talking?" Frank asked.

"The guy who's in charge of all the Children of Noah on the *Ark*, and one of the crew. I might not have paid any attention, except that they were skulking all by themselves up on the boat deck and talking kind of low, as if they didn't want anyone to hear them. They didn't seem to realize I was sprawled out on the deck right nearby, or maybe they thought I was asleep."

Buzz said that his interest was aroused by the oddness of the conversation. "They seemed to be talking partly in code. For instance, two or three times I heard them say something that sounded like *Cara-Vojjo*, whatever that means. And they also kept referring to the 'Flower Basket Scene.' Whatever they were talking about, it seemed to have something to do with the cult agent's houseboat in Bayport."

"What cult agent?" asked Joe.

"The guy who drums up odd jobs for the culties—I mean the ones who come ashore during the day to work."

Frank and Joe exchanged puzzled glances. Neither could imagine what the conversation might have been about nor what the code words might mean.

But suddenly Tony Prito spoke up. "That first one sounds like an Italian name—Caravaggio." He spelled it for the others.

Frank frowned, then snapped his fingers. "I've got a hunch I've heard that name before!" he exclaimed. "And I bet I know just where to find out for sure!"

As soon as they had tied up at the boat landing, Tony led the boys a little ways along the waterfront. "I think that's the houseboat Buzz heard them talking about," he said, pointing to a craft that was moored to a dock nearby.

"You're right!" cried Joe. "Look at that design stenciled on the side, Frank!"

The design portrayed a bird in flight with a leafy branch in its mouth, *the same as the dove and olive-branch symbol on the amulet!*

Frank asked the others to keep an eye on the houseboat. Meanwhile he hurried to the Hardy boys' car and drove to the Howard Museum, where he spoke to the art curator, a slender, wispy-haired man with rimless, pinch-nose glasses.

"Mr. Scath, am I mistaken in thinking there was an Italian painter named Caravaggio?"

"No, indeed, Frank, you're quite right. In fact there were two painters by that name. You're probably thinking of the more famous one, Michelangelo da Caravaggio, who lived during the late fifteen hundreds—had a very melodramatic style with lots of light and shadow."

Frank socked his fist into the palm of his other hand. "I knew I'd heard that name somewhere!"

"Most likely in the news," the curator said. "A painting by Caravaggio was sold at auction just a few days ago for an exceptionally high price. It was titled *Girl with Flower Basket*."

Frank sped back to the harbor excitedly. Joe and his two companions reported that the cult agent had left the houseboat and driven off in his car fifteen minutes earlier.

"Wow!" Joe exclaimed on hearing his brother's news. "If that conversation Buzz overheard means what it sounds like, there may be evidence on the houseboat that would help Dad get the goods on Noah Norvel!"

"And now's our chance to find out!" said Frank.

Buzz and Tony had no intention of being left out of the adventure. They tagged along eagerly as the Hardys boldly went aboard the craft. The agent, apparently unworried about any risk of a burglary, had left the houseboat unlocked.

"There it is!" Joe gasped. In the main room of the houseboat hung a large painting. It showed a barefoot young peasant girl in the marketplace, holding a basketful of flowers!

Then a voice snapped: "You thieves!"

# 16

## A Baited Trap

The Hardy boys and their two friends whirled around as they heard the voice behind them. An angry looking, red-faced man was standing in the doorway.

"It's the cult agent!" Tony hissed out of the corner of his mouth to Frank. The older Hardy boy had already guessed as much.

The agent glared at them furiously. He seemed to be almost trembling with rage. Frank thought he detected a trace of alarm in the man's expression as well.

"How dare you young punks break into my houseboat!" the agent ranted.

"We didn't break in, we walked in," Joe said coolly.

"You realize I could have you all arrested for attempted burglary?"

"I doubt that," said Frank.

His remark seemed to provoke the agent still further. "Get off my boat," the red-faced man stormed, "before I call the police!"

Like his brother, Frank had decided that their best tactic was bluffing. "Sure, we'll leave," he replied calmly. "But don't let that stop you. Go right ahead and call the police if you think you've got a case against us."

The Hardys led the way across the deck of the houseboat and back onto the pier, followed by Tony and Buzz. They heard the door slam behind them.

The four youths paused at a safe distance from the houseboat, in case the cult agent might still be watching them furtively.

"Looks like we've got Noah and his stooges dead to rights!" Joe exulted.

"It sure does," Frank agreed. "Remember what Dad told us about that stolen-art racket?"

"Every time something's taken, a fake or forgery is left in its place."

"Right! So if that picture we saw just now is the Caravaggio painting called *Girl with Flower Basket*, then the one sold at auction must have been a forgery. The two were probably switched just before the auction!"

"I'd say you guys are the ones who ought to be calling the police," put in Tony with a dry chuckle. "You might even get a reward for finding the real painting!"

"If we did, we'd split it four ways, with you and Buzz," Frank declared. "But I think we should check with Dad first. We sure wouldn't want to go spoiling any plan of action he may have for dealing with Noah."

Joe was of the same opinion. Nevertheless, after managing to contact their father by a long-distance phone call, both brothers were somewhat surprised when he advised extreme caution.

"Sit tight until Sam Radley gets there," Fenton Hardy told his sons. "He'll bring you instructions on just what to do."

Frank and Joe and their two companions settled down to wait in the Hardy boys' car. It was parked in a spot that enabled them to keep watch on the houseboat, in case any attempt was made to sneak the painting away.

After an hour's wait, Tony Prito reluctantly announced that he had to go. He was due at work at an excavation site where his father's construction company was pouring the foundations for a new building. "Be sure and let me know how things come out!" he said.

"We will," Frank promised. "And thanks a lot for

taking us out to the *Ark* in the *Napoli*."

Almost another hour went by before Sam Radley finally drove up and parked alongside the Hardy boys' car. He brought with him a short, stout man with a bristling reddish mustache. "This is Mr. Hacker of the art auction gallery that sold the Caravaggio picture," Sam introduced him to the boys. "He's an expert on Italian painting of that period, so he can tell us whether that picture on the houseboat is the real McCoy."

"How are you going to get a look at it?" Joe asked, after shaking hands with Hacker. "That employment agent for the cult is still aboard."

"Your dad's got that all figured out," Radley said, "and he's also talked to Police Chief Collig, who's promised to cooperate. But we'll need one of your high-school gang to pose as a new recruit for the cult."

Joe glanced at his brother. "How about Biff Hooper? He even shaved his head so he could go to the comic book party as Cue Ball, remember?"

Frank grinned. "Perfect! That'll make him look all the more convincing. He can pretend he shaved himself bald on purpose, just so he could join the Children of Noah!"

Biff readily agreed to help out when the Hardys called him. Then they stood by while Sam Radley transmitted exact instructions over the phone.

Twenty minutes later, the Hardys' tall, rangy chum arrived on the dock. Walking straight up to where the houseboat was moored, he knocked loudly on the door. The cult agent opened up.

"I want to find out how to join the Children of Noah," Biff announced and started to shoulder his way inside.

"Hold it, kid!" the agent retorted suspiciously. "Nobody comes barging in here uninvited! I don't even know who you are!"

"My name's Biff Hooper, if that makes any difference. You think I'd have shaved my hair off already if I weren't serious about joining? Come on, let me in! How soon can we go out to the *Ark?*"

"I've already told you, nobody comes barging aboard uninvited!" the agent growled. "Just stay put on the dock till the Children of Noah decide whether or not they want to accept you!"

His face was turning red again, and as he spoke, the agent tried to push Biff back out of the doorway.

"Don't go shoving me around!" Biff protested. As if to emphasize his words, the husky footballer pushed back with a strong, stiff-armed shove of his own.

The angry agent responded in kind. His temper seemed to grow shorter with each exchange. Before long, the two were engaged in a noisy scuffle,

138

which soon threatened to turn into an out-and-out fistfight.

In their angry confrontation, neither noticed the policeman who came striding toward them. "All right, enough, you two! What's going on here?" he demanded.

"This punk's trying to force his way onto my houseboat!" the cult agent charged loudly.

"I came to join the Children of Noah, and he started shoving me around!" Biff retorted.

Soon he and the agent were hurling accusations back and forth and arguing as furiously as they had been scuffling a few moments before.

"You're both under arrest for disturbing the peace!" the policeman broke in, shouting to make himself heard. "So pipe down, both of you, and come along with me!"

After summoning help by walkie-talkie, the officer herded his two charges into a squad car, which then drove off to the police station.

The three boys, who had watched the whole episode from the car, burst out laughing at Biff's highly convincing performance.

"Never mind all that," grinned Sam Radley. "Now's our chance to slip aboard so Mr. Hacker can get a good look at that painting."

The Hardy boys and Buzz Barton waited on the dock while Fenton Hardy's operative escorted the

art expert aboard the houseboat. Ten minutes went by, then fifteen.

"Boy, that guy from the gallery must really be giving the picture a good going-over!" Joe said some time later, with a glance at his watch.

Frank nodded anxiously. "They'd better hurry, or Noah's stooge might get back in time to catch them!"

Actually, Police Chief Collig himself was dealing with the two disturbers of the peace and was doing so in somewhat leisurely fashion. At first he had let them cool their heels in a waiting room at the police station before he found time to interview them personally. Then he questioned each of them at length about their quarrel on the dock.

"Well now, I don't think this incident is serious enough to warrant an arrest," he announced finally. "Seems to me both of you had reason to get a little huffy, but that's no excuse to start beating each other up. If you'll both shake hands, I'm prepared to dismiss the charges."

Grumpily the cult agent and Biff obeyed. By the time the agent returned to the dock there was no sign that anyone had entered the houseboat in his absence.

Meanwhile, Sam Radley and Mr. Hacker were informing the three boys about the results of the art expert's inspection of the painting.

"It's definitely not a Caravaggio," said Hacker. "I'd rate it as a pretty fair copy of the picture we sold at auction, but it would never stand up to close examination."

Frank and Joe looked at each other in chagrin and then at Sam Radley.

"I'll bet Noah and his stooges didn't have that made overnight," said Frank. "It would take some time to make that good a copy, wouldn't it, Mr. Hacker?"

The art expert nodded. "Yes, I would say a few days, anyhow, although some forgers work pretty fast."

"Which means they may have been planning to heist the original," said Radley, "if that's what you're getting at, Frank."

"Right, Sam. But that doesn't alter the fact that they sure fooled me and Joe. I'll bet the whole thing was a carefully planned setup, just to trick us into making a false accusation, and then later on, they could sue us for plenty!"

"I'm afraid you're right," the operative agreed. "Not only that, but if your dad did bring other charges against them later on, a false arrest now would badly weaken his case."

"Thank goodness Dad kept us from falling into their trap!" said Joe, trying to look at the bright side.

The Hardy boys drove Buzz Barton home to Shoreham, then headed back rather glumly to their own house in Bayport. A plump figure bounced down from the porch to greet them as they pulled into the driveway on Elm Street. It was Chet Morton.

"Guess what!" the chubby youth exclaimed.

"We gave up already," said Joe, "so tell us. What's the big news?"

"Star Comix just bought my cartoon story!"

# 17

## Night Flight

"Hey, that's great, Chet! Congratulations!" Joe cried, getting out of the car and greeting the fat boy with a hearty handshake. "When did you find out?"

"I just got a call from New York this afternoon!"

"Looks like you're on your way to fame and fortune!" said Frank, adding a congratulatory handshake of his own.

Both the Hardy boys were tickled over Chet's good luck. Besides being pleased for their friend's sake, the news helped to cheer them up after the somewhat discouraging outcome of their houseboat adventure.

"Say, I think this deserves a celebration!" Frank went on. He told Chet briefly about the flower-

144

basket painting and explained that they had promised to take Biff Hooper to a steak-and-chips dinner and an early movie, in reward for his help in making it possible for the art expert to inspect the painting on the houseboat. "Why don't you come with us, Chet? The treat's on us!"

"In that case, how can I refuse?" chortled the budding cartoonist.

Because of his summer job as a milkman's helper, Biff had to be in bed promptly every evening. So it was only a few minutes after nine-thirty when the Hardy boys returned home that night.

Aunt Gertrude met them as they walked in the door. "You had two calls while you were out!"

"From whom, Aunt Gertrude?" Frank asked.

"One was from the director of the Comic Art Museum, and the other was from that fellow in the comic book business, Micky Rudd. They sounded urgent. I think you'd better call them back right now!"

Frank and Joe shot a quick glance at each other, both boys smothering grins as they did so. From Miss Hardy's somewhat nagging, peckish manner, they could tell that she was eaten up with curiosity over the cause of the unusual nighttime calls. As usual with their detective cases, she was keeping in close touch with their work on the Apeman mystery and the disappearance of Sue Linwood.

"Okay, Aunty," Frank replied. "We'll call them back right now. Did you get their numbers?"

"Naturally!" From her severe tone of voice, the tall, bony woman sounded almost insulted at the very idea that she might be guilty of such an oversight.

Frank chuckled silently as he dialed the museum director's number on the telephone in the front hall. Both he and Joe were aware that their aunt was hovering close by, listening with sharp ears and keeping an eye on developments through her gold-rimmed spectacles.

"This is Frank Hardy, returning your call, Mr. Tappan," said the elder Hardy boy as the director's voice came on the line.

"Oh, yes. I thought you fellows might be interested in something we discovered just before closing time this evening."

"We certainly are, sir, if it has anything to do with this Apeman impostor."

"I suspect it may. If you recall, you were inquiring about some work by an artist named Archie Frome, which was donated to the museum, and we found that some of it was missing."

"Yes, sir," Frank responded. "What about it?"

"Well, the damage caused by the vandal was cleaned up first thing this morning. But this evening we found a very odd drawing lying on the floor in the main display room."

146

"What sort of drawing? And what's so odd about it?"

"For one thing, it's signed by Archie Frome, at least it bears the usual signature that appears on all his artwork. But I'm sure the drawing's a fake!"

"How come?"

"I know Frome's stuff very well," Mr. Tappan said, "and this doesn't look like his work at all. It's nothing like his usual style."

"What's it a drawing *of?*" Frank asked. "I mean, what sort of a sketch is it?"

"It's a drawing of the Apeman, just like the comic book Apeman or the character on TV. It shows him going into a cave."

Joe, who was listening in on the conversation at Frank's elbow, gave a low whistle.

Frank, too, was keenly intrigued by the museum director's strange discovery. "That may be important, Mr. Tappan! Joe and I had better drive up and take a look at it tomorrow."

"Fine! I'll expect you."

"How's that for a weird twist," Frank said as he hung up.

"How can I offer an opinion when I don't even know what you're talking about!" Miss Hardy cut in. Her rather sharply pointed nose seemed to be twitching with curiosity.

Frank grinned and relayed the odd news he had received from Mr. Tappan.

"Hmph! Sounds to me like a *planted* clue!" his aunt opined shrewdly.

Frank was startled and impressed. The thought, which had also flickered through his own mind, certainly fitted in with the fact that the damage from the vandal's raid had already been cleaned up. "You know, you could be right, at that, Aunt Gertrude," he mused.

"Of course I could be right!" she snapped. "What's so unusual about that?"

"Er, nothing, Aunty." He smiled. "I was just thinking."

"Good! I'm glad to hear it. In my opinion, the secret of successful crime detection is *always* good, clear thinking."

"Yes, ma'am."

Frank's next call was to Micky Rudd, who answered so promptly that he gave the impression he was sitting by the telephone, waiting for it to ring.

"What's up, Mr. Rudd?" Frank asked.

"Plenty! At least, that's my hunch!" As usual, the editor-publisher's voice sounded tense and excited, as though the call had caught him in the midst of a comic book crisis. As a matter of fact, Frank reflected, that might be exactly what the Apeman impostor was causing at Star Comix. "I've just been promised a tip," Rudd went on, "as to where we can find the hideout of this nut who's been posing as the Apeman!"

"Who promised it?"

"How do I know? The tipster didn't give me his name! What I mean is," Rudd explained, slowing down his machine-gun style of speaking, "I got this anonymous call shortly after dinnertime. The voice at the other end of the line said if I'd stay close to the phone tonight, he'd call back later and tell me where to find the fake Apeman's cave hideout. When I asked who was speaking, he just growled, *'None of your business!'* and hung up!"

"Wait a minute!" Frank broke in, picking up some of Rudd's excitement. "When your caller promised this tip, did he use those exact two words—*cave hideout?*"

"That's right. Why?"

"Well, sir, it may be just coincidence, but that ties in with something else that came up tonight." Frank told him about the drawing found at the Comic Art Museum, which showed the Apeman going into a *cave.*

Micky Rudd was immediately excited. "Follow that up!" he exclaimed, like a general barking out orders to his troops. "You and your brother better get up there right away!"

"You mean *tonight?*" Frank gasped, lifting his eyebrows in a startled look at Joe and Aunt Gertrude.

"Sure, while the clue's fresh! If this anonymous call I got means anything, then there must be some connection! Maybe that drawing'll give some hint of where the cave's located. Once you get up there to the museum and take a look at it, give me another ring and I'll tell you if I've had any more news from the tipster!"

Neither Hardy boy was enthusiastic about starting out on such a lengthy trip at so late an hour. However, after checking a map, Joe phoned the Ace Air Service at Bayport airfield and arranged for a charter flight to the Westchester County Airport, which the map showed was not far from the Comic Art Museum. The Ace Air Service was operated by a pilot named Jack Wayne, who also acted as Mr. Hardy's personal pilot when the detective needed him on his investigations.

Luckily, after landing in Westchester, the boys were able to obtain a car from a twenty-four-hour rental agency. They drove swiftly to the home of Gerald Tappan, whom they had alerted by a telephone call from Bayport and who had promised to wait up for their visit.

With keen interest, Frank and Joe studied the drawing he handed them. It was done in pen and ink on white paper.

"You're quite sure this is not Frome's work?" Frank asked the museum director.

"Positive! In fact, the more I look at it, the more I'm inclined to think that it was done by an amateur—or at least the inking was."

"How come, sir?" Joe asked with a puzzled frown.

"It's a little hard to explain, but—well, the inked lines aren't quite true. They're not done with assurance, whereas the Apeman's figure itself seems to be drawn with professional skill."

"You mean, a professional artist might have drawn the picture in pencil, and then it was inked over by an amateur?"

"Right." Tappan explained that, in comic book work, the penciling and inking were often done by entirely different artists. "It may be," he added, "that whoever did this picture *traced* the Apeman from a comic book and then inked the tracing."

"H'm, that's interesting. Another funny thing," Frank mused aloud, "is that the face of the Apeman in this drawing seems to look like somebody I've seen. But I can't figure out who."

"Same here!" Joe exclaimed. "He reminds me of somebody, too!"

After asking Mr. Tappan if he might use the phone, Frank called Micky Rudd in New York City. Rudd's voice was seething with excitement again as he answered the Hardy boy's query as to whether he had heard any more from the mysterious tipster.

"I sure did! He called back about ten minutes ago," the comic book editor reported, "and this time he gave me exact directions on where to find that nut's cave hideout!"

151

# *18*

## *The Sleeping Ogre*

"Let's have the directions he gave you, Mr. Rudd."
Whipping out a pencil, Frank jotted them down,
then said, "Okay, we'll check out the tip right away,
sir!"

Gerald Tappan was startled by the news, and Joe
was almost as excited as Rudd himself had sounded
on the telephone. The museum director read over
the instructions on how to reach the cave, then
brought out a road map and showed the boys that
the location was only a ten- or fifteen-minute drive
from his house.

Frank stood up. "Of course there is a chance that
this is a trap," he said. "If you don't hear from us
within a couple of hours, Mr. Tappan, will you
please notify the police?"

Tappan nodded. "Be careful, will you?"

The boys left and soon were whizzing along the highway through the nighttime darkness.

"Think there's any chance we'll find the guy who's been posing as the Apeman?" Joe asked, shooting a glance at his brother.

Frank, who was at the wheel, responded with a shrug. "Could be. Just from the timing of those calls to Rudd, I have a hunch the tipster knows there's something in that cave right now. Or someone!"

Both boys felt a twinge of nervousness at the prospect of facing the huge, savage brute who had tried to wreck the Alfresco Disco. He might be a fake as far as impersonating the Apeman was concerned, but there was no doubt about the size of his muscles! And this time there would be just the two of them, alone and unarmed, facing his fury!

Tappan had told them to watch for a certain highway intersection, followed by an expressway turnoff. About a mile and a half beyond this, the ground on the right of the road would rise in a steep hillside, and among a clump of trees near the top, according to Rudd's telephoned instructions, they would find the cave opening.

"Here we are!" Frank muttered presently. He slowed, turned off the road, and braked to a halt.

The boys got out and started up the hillside, each carrying a flashlight. No sounds of traffic reached their ears from the highway below. At this time of night the silence was intense, broken only by a faint, sleepy chirp of crickets and the scuff of their own footsteps trudging up the slope.

"There's the cave opening!" Joe whispered as his flashlight beam picked out a yawning recess in the ground just ahead.

Frank put out a hand to caution his brother. Silently they tiptoed to the mouth of the cave. Joe stifled a gasp as Frank shone his flashlight inside.

A huge figure lay sprawled just a few yards from the entrance. The man was clad in a brief fur garment and had his head resting on one crooked arm. His back was turned to the boys, and from the heavy snores issuing over his shoulder, he was obviously fast asleep.

"Stand by for a quick retreat!" Frank whispered to Joe. Then he scooped up a handful of grit and gravel and flung it at the sleeping giant.

The figure briefly twitched and groaned. Then the snoring resumed.

Frank picked up several larger pebbles and tried again, this time with explosive results! The man grunted and sat bolt upright. Then as his sleep-dulled eyes became aware of the flashlight glow, he bellowed and leaped to his feet, whirling around as he did so.

He blinked in the dazzling glare, and his jaw dropped open in a stupid gape.

"Gallopin' grasshoppers!" Joe gasped. "It's Zack Amboy!"

"And all of a sudden I know who that Apeman in the drawing reminds me of!" Frank murmured.

"You're right! His face looks like Zack's!"

"Who's out there?" Amboy demanded. "What's going on?"

The two young sleuths shifted their flashlight beams so he could see them, and Frank said, "We're the Hardy boys, Zack, Frank and Joe. Remember us?"

"Sure! You bet I do! B-B-But ... where am I? ... How did I get here?"

"That's just what we were going to ask you," said Joe.

The muscular giant seemed dazed and utterly bewildered. He shambled forward and peered out at the tree-covered slope, then glanced back at the spot where he had been lying. "This is a cave!" he mumbled, as if he were just becoming aware of the fact.

"That's right," Frank said evenly, his tone expressing neither belief nor disbelief in Zack's amazement.

"Well, I'll be a monkey's uncle!" Amboy blurted.

"You sure could be in that getup," Joe said with a hint of amusement. "Some people might think that's the Apeman's costume you're wearing!"

155

"The *Apeman?*" Zack Amboy echoed in a troubled voice. "Now wait a minute! You guys don't think I'm that nut who's been going around posing as the Apeman, do you?"

"Why don't you tell *us?*" said Frank. "Are you or aren't you?"

"Of course I'm not!"

"Then what're you doing in that fur getup?" Joe asked.

"How do I know?" Zack put one hand to the top of his head and added, "Look! Do I have a big mop of hair like the Apeman's got? Does my jaw stick way out like his does?"

"All that's just a matter of makeup. You're still wearing the right costume for the role."

"Wait a minute!" Frank broke in. "If you don't know how you happen to be wearing that fur suit, can you at least tell us how you got here?"

"I don't know that, either!" Zack's voice came out as a strange mixture of a wail and a bellow. It might have sounded comical coming from so large and powerful a man, had the look on his face not been dead serious.

"What *do* you remember? Anything at all?"

"Not much." Zack paused, rubbing his head again and scowling. "Say, what day is this?" he exclaimed suddenly.

When Frank told him, the muscle man nodded.

"That's what I thought . . . Well, let's see. I—I seem to remember leaving the house this morning . . . and I've got a hunch I worked out at the gym . . . but it's all pretty hazy."

The Hardy boys exchanged doubtful glances.

"You've gotta believe me!" Zack pleaded. "I'm not that loony who goes around acting like the Apeman and busting things up! I swear I'm not! Somebody's trying to frame me! They just planted me here in this getup!"

Again Frank and Joe looked at each other. "It's possible that someone slipped him some knockout drops," Joe theorized, "or maybe a drug that wiped out his memory."

"Okay," Frank said. "I suppose it could have happened that way. But you'll have to admit, Zack, the way things stand right now you look pretty suspicious."

"How did you guys find me?"

"A telephone tip," Frank said tersely, not wanting to give away anything more than necessary.

Zack not only made no effort to get away, he meekly promised to hold himself available for questioning by the police. He even asked the Hardys to give him a lift to some place where he might get a ride back to his home in Brooklyn.

"We're headed for the Westchester County Airport," said Joe.

157

"That'll do fine!" Zack said gratefully. "Maybe I can get some mechanic's duds there to cover up with."

On the way to the airport, Zack kept trying to convince the boys of his innocence. "Would I strand myself way out here in the boondocks," he argued, "without a car or a bike? Or even any street clothes!"

"For all we know, you might've been expecting someone to pick you up," Joe pointed out.

"But why should I even *want* to go around posing as the Apeman and getting everyone sore at me? I've got nothing to do with that Apeman television program! All I know about it is what I've heard from Rollo Eckert!"

The Hardys were immediately intrigued by Zack's mention of the weight lifter with the broken leg whom they had met at the Olympic Gymnasium. Both remembered him saying that he was from California.

"What does Rollo Eckert know about 'The Apeman' TV show?" Frank asked as they drove along.

"Plenty! At least he knows a lot more than I do!" Zack replied. "He was hoping to land the starring role on that program. In fact, he was one of the two finalists for the part."

"Are you sure about that?"

"Sure, I'm sure! He only lost out to Dante Mazzola at the last minute. The casting of the show was big news among top body builders all over the country."

Jack Wayne, who had evidently been on the lookout for the Hardy boys, waved excitedly as they pulled up at the airport. "I just got a flash from your dad about ten minutes ago over my plane radio!" he reported.

"What's up, Jack?" Frank inquired anxiously. "Anything wrong?"

"He said to tell you that Noah Norvel's mansion was raided by the Apeman impostor a little more than an hour ago."

The Hardy boys were startled by the news. From the stricken look on Zack Amboy's face, it was clear that the fur-clad strong man realized that this development placed him under even deeper suspicion than before.

The airport lay about midway between the Comic Art Museum and Noah's mansion, which meant they could drive to the latter in about fifteen minutes.

Frank said, "Do you mind waiting around for us awhile longer, Jack, while we check out what happened at Noah Norvel's?"

"No problem. From what your dad said, I expected you'd want to go there." With a grin, the pilot jerked his thumb toward Zack Amboy and added, "While you're gone, I'll see if I can rustle up a suit of coveralls to fit this bruiser."

"Great! Thanks, Jack. Also, please call Mr. Tappan for us and tell him we're okay. Here's the number."

The Hardys were soon on their way to the cult leader's mansion. They found several scout cars drawn up in the long driveway while policemen searched the grounds for clues. The house was ablaze with lights. Frank and Joe had no difficulty gaining entrance, and they learned that their father had asked the FBI to notify the local police of their probable arrival.

Noah, however, was in a towering rage and glared at the Hardy boys suspiciously.

"How many people were here with you at the time of the raid?" Frank asked him.

"Six of my children, if it's any of your business!"

"You mean your *own* children or members of your cult?"

"Children of Noah!" Norvel snapped.

"What about servants?" put in Joe.

"The children act as my aides and also do whatever household work is necessary."

The bearded cult leader's response drew scornful looks from both the Hardys, who realized this meant, in effect, that Noah used the teenage culties as his personal slaves.

Under prodding from Lieutenant Allen, the policeman in charge of the case, Norvel repeated his story of what had happened. He said that the fake Apeman had broken open the front door and come bursting into the mansion. He had knocked out the three male culties when they tried to resist him and had gassed two of the girls unconscious with a chloroform-soaked rag.

Noah himself had been roughed up and tied. "I couldn't even call the police till I managed to pull one of my wrists free and got loose from the ropes," he related angrily. "Meanwhile, that maniac rampaged around, smashing furniture as you see, and ransacked my private study!"

When Frank asked to interview the cultie servants, the three youths who had been knocked out and the two girls who had been chloroformed were brought in. The sixth cultie, who was another teenage girl, the Hardys were now told, had been dragged off by the fake Apeman as a hostage.

"What was her name?" Joe exclaimed suddenly.

"Sue Linwood, as if you didn't know!" Norvel ranted.

Frank responded with a hard look of his own. "How come none of your outside guards were able to stop the intruder?" he demanded.

"Because they were decoyed away and kayoed, one by one, which I'm sure is no news to you!"

"Just what is that supposed to mean?" Frank exploded.

Instead of answering, Noah flung up his arms in a melodramatic gesture of disgust and turned to the police captain. "I've had enough of this farce!" he exploded. "I'm willing to bet these two and their father were behind tonight's raid—as cover-up for a plot to snatch the Linwood girl away from my control!"

"You're crazy!" Joe blazed at the cult leader.

"Am I? Then how does it happen you were seen less than an hour ago in company with the fake Apeman?"

# 19

## Hidden Duo

The Hardy boys were caught off guard by Noah Norvel's sudden accusing question.

Frank recovered first. "How would you know where we were or whom we were seen with, if you were tied up here at your house?"

"For your information," the cult leader gloated, "I was tipped off by an anonymous phone call just before the police arrived."

"Very convenient," Joe needled. "If you don't even know who called, there's no way anyone can check up on your story, is there?"

Noah's face flushed angrily. "You two are the ones who'd better start worrying about having your story checked up on!" he rasped.

Police Lieutenant Allen eyed the Hardy boys

keenly. "Is this true, what Mr. Norvel says," he cut in, "about you fellows being with this phony Apeman?"

"Not exactly, sir," Frank replied. "We were with someone who was dressed in a costume like the Apeman's, and being a weight lifter, he also happens to be muscled like the Apeman. But that doesn't prove he's the vandal who's been posing as the Apeman—in fact, I'm convinced he's *not*. Don't you agree, Joe?"

"Definitely. What's more, we have reason to believe he may have been drugged tonight, Lieutenant. It looks as though someone deliberately tried to frame him."

"What's this muscle man's name?" Allen asked.

"Zack Amboy," Joe said. "He's promised to hold himself available for questioning."

"H'm." The policeman frowned. "He may not be the only one who'll have to be questioned. In view of what's happened tonight and what you've just told me, you two may have to testify before a grand jury yourselves. Normally I'd be inclined to hold you both as material witnesses. However, because of your father's reputation and the fine detective work you fellows have done on your own, I'll let you go for now, that is, if you'll agree to cooperate anytime we need you up here, to help carry out our investigation."

164

"You have our word, sir," the Hardys promised. Despite Noah Norvel's angry remonstrances, Lieutenant Allen allowed them to leave the mansion.

The boys sped back to the Westchester County Airport, where Jack Wayne and Zack Amboy were waiting, avid for news of the night's events.

Frank and Joe filled them in. Then the elder Hardy boy asked Zack, "Any idea where Rollo Eckert is staying while he's here in the East?"

"Sure. He's renting a seaside cottage not far from Bayport, where you guys live. It's right on the outskirts of Shoreham."

"*Shoreham?*" echoed the Hardys.

As Zack nodded, Frank asked, "Have you actually seen his cottage?"

"Yeah, I've been there." Zack explained that Eckert had brought no exercise equipment with him when he left California. So he had placed an order through the Olympic Gym for a pair of fixed-weight dumbbells, which he could work out with regularly, in spite of his broken leg. Zack, who enjoyed sailing, had volunteered to bring the dumbbells from the gym to the cottage on his boat, and Eckert had accepted the offer.

"Can you tell us exactly how to find the cottage?" Frank pursued.

"Sure, I can draw you a little map. Why, are you guys gonna look him up tomorrow?"

"Sooner than that. We might even pay him a visit tonight."

Before taking off, the Hardy boys tried to call their father to report developments and ask his advice, using the radio transceiver in Jack Wayne's airplane, *Skyhappy Sal*. But they could get no response.

"Any idea where Dad was calling from when you talked to him tonight?" Joe asked the pilot.

"Long Island, I think. He said he was checking out some important leads on a case, and he wanted to know if I could pick him up at MacArthur Airport tomorrow, in case he needed to get back in a hurry."

Frank said, "If we can't raise him before we land at Bayport, could you fly to MacArthur tonight and try to locate him, Jack?"

"Sure thing."

Zack Amboy, who was eager to clear himself of suspicion, volunteered to go along and help in any way possible. The Hardy boys gladly accepted, feeling that Jack Wayne might need assistance in tracking down their father on Long Island.

As they had feared, the boys were unable to contact Mr. Hardy before *Skyhappy Sal* landed at the Bayport airfield. Frank then jotted a hasty note, which he handed to the pilot.

"Please keep trying to raise Dad. Use the emergency call letters on your way to MacArthur. And if you do get a response or find him on Long Island, give him that information."

"Okay, Frank."

The boys waved good-bye as the pilot and Zack Amboy took off again. Then they hurried to their car in the airport parking lot and were soon heading for Shoreham.

Skirting the business section of town, they took the road that led to the adjoining beach area. Here they parked and made their way on foot across a rise of sand dunes toward the water.

Rollo Eckert's rented cottage was isolated from other homes along the shore. It was located on a sandy spit jutting out from the rest of the beach. Light glowed from its curtained windows, and two cars were parked in front of the house, one of them a large, expensive-looking limousine.

"Good thing we didn't drive right up to Eckert's front door," Joe muttered to his brother. "This way, we can give him a little surprise."

Frank nodded grimly. "Right, and if we surprise him enough, maybe we can learn more than what he wants to tell us!"

The boys approached the cottage and Frank knocked lightly. After a moment the door opened just wide enough for Rollo Eckert to peer out.

His jaw dropped wide open and he gasped as he

recognized the Hardy boys. Before he could slam the door in their faces, Frank and Joe shoved it wide open. Eckert fell back in dismay, and the boys saw that he had neither a cast on his leg nor a crutch under his arm!

"Did your fracture heal up all of a sudden?" Joe asked sarcastically.

"N-No! I—I mean it didn't heal all of a sudden," Rollo Eckert stammered. "It's b-been mending gradually. The doctor just took off my cast today."

"And I suppose you're keeping those two neat halves of the cast for souvenirs!" Frank needled, pointing toward a pair of long white objects visible on a nearby table.

Eckert was dressed in shorts and a tank top, which amply revealed his deep chest and muscular build. His face seemed to be mottled red and white with rage and guilt.

But the Hardys were no longer observing his expression. They had suddenly noticed certain other items. One was a fur garment flung over the back of a chair. Another was a bushy black wig lying on the table near the fake plaster cast.

Frank strode over to pick up a third object. It was a built-up rubber face mask, much thicker in the jaw and forehead areas than in others.

"So this is what gives you that heavy-jawed beetling-browed Apeman look!" the elder Hardy boy exclaimed.

"I didn't make that," Eckert blustered foolishly. "It belongs to the TV film studio that's shooting 'The Apeman' series."

"But you're the one who's been wearing it!" Frank charged. "In fact, you've been using this costume as a disguise so you could pose as the Apeman when you vandalized that movie theater and the Alfresco Disco and all the other places you've raided!"

Rollo Eckert's face was twisted with emotion. He struggled for several moments to get his voice under control. Then his shoulders seemed to slump as he mumbled, "Okay, I'll admit I was the fake Apeman. B-But I wasn't trying to hurt anyone! It was just a—a prank to get even!"

"For losing out in the competition for the starring role," Frank prompted.

Rollo nodded hopelessly. He scarcely seemed to notice the fact that Joe was silently edging away across the room. "I intended to quit," he blurted, "after that night you guys almost caught me at the park disco. But then I got blackmailed into pulling those raids on the Comic Art Museum and Noah Norvel's mansion."

"You mean—blackmailed by Vern Kelso?" As Frank spoke, he signaled his brother with one hand.

Joe flung open the door leading to the back room of the small cottage. His action revealed two startling figures. One was Sue Linwood, blindfolded,

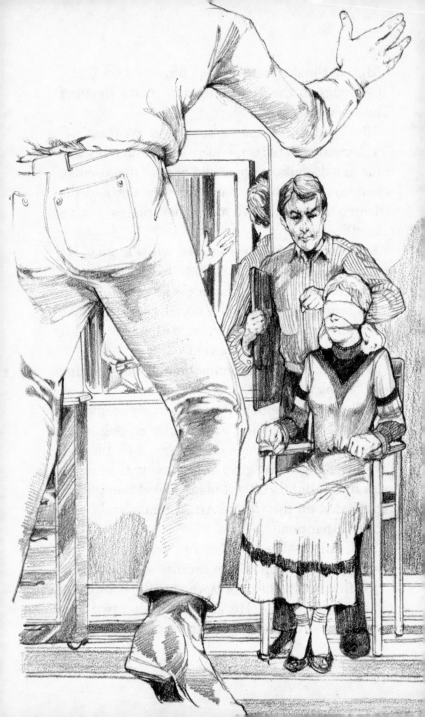

gagged, and tied to a chair! A man loomed over her in a menacing fashion, as if threatening to harm her if she tried to thump her feet or make any other noise to attract attention.

The man was Vern Kelso. Under one arm he was clutching the large file folder stolen from the crateful of Archie Frome's work at the Comic Art Museum! Both Hardy boys recognized it at once from its similarity to the other folders they had seen in the crate.

Kelso burst into a loud, raging harangue. "How did you two nosy brats know I was in here?" he screamed while Joe set to work untying Sue Linwood's tightly knotted gag.

"It wasn't hard to figure, especially with that limousine sitting outside," Frank retorted. "For one thing, you deliberately lied to us about the competition for the Apeman role on TV. You were trying to cover up the fact that Rollo only lost out at the last minute, so we wouldn't suspect him. Joe and I also told you about our meeting with Zack Amboy, which made him the obvious choice for a fall guy to be arrested in place of Rollo."

Kelso's bravado seemed to collapse when he realized how thoroughly the Hardy boys had uncovered his part in the Apeman mystery. Frank and Joe guessed that he also assumed they had alerted their father and the police before coming to the cottage, and they let him go on thinking so.

"Believe it or not, this whole mess wasn't my fault!" Kelso fumed, striding back and forth as he gave vent to his emotion.

"Oh, no? Then whose fault was it?" Frank prodded.

"Micky Rudd, if you want the whole truth!" As he spoke, Kelso abruptly opened the large art folder that he had carried with him when he ducked into the back room on hearing the boys' knock.

After leafing through the contents of the folder, Kelso plucked out several pages of artwork, which he held up to show Frank and Joe. To their astonishment, they saw that they contained the drawings for a comic book story featuring a character just like the Apeman!

"Leapin' lizards!" exclaimed Joe, suddenly catching on. "You mean Micky Rudd *stole* the Apeman character from Archie Frome?"

"You guessed it," Kelso replied grimly. "Several years ago, Frome brought this story to Star Comix. Rudd turned it down. But later on, in an emergency, when he needed a story in a hurry to fill out one of his comic books, he pirated Frome's yarn. He had it drawn by one of his staff artists, but it still had the same plot as Frome's story, and the Apeman looked practically the same way Frome had drawn him.

172

"As it turned out, the Apeman made a big hit with the readers of Star Comix, so Rudd was forced to run more stories about him. Finally, the company began putting out a regular monthly comic book titled 'The Apeman.'

"At first Rudd worried that Frome might discover the theft of his character. But when the artist failed to complain and turned to illustrating children's books, Rudd began to relax and feel that there would be no trouble over his plagiarism.

"Eventually," Kelso continued, "a Hollywood producer bought the television rights to the Apeman from Star Comix, and the Federated Broadcasting System purchased the show at my own suggestion."

"Didn't Rudd realize he was laying himself open to a possible lawsuit?" put in Joe.

"Certainly! But he was too greedy to pass up such a deal. Besides, Rudd isn't the sole owner of Star Comix, and the other owners of the company wouldn't have *let* him turn down the television offer."

Frank said, "But I bet that's what prompted him to try and steal the artwork for the original story from Frome's studio, right?"

Kelso confirmed this. "At first," he said, "Rudd was relieved to hear of Frome's death, thinking that now his guilty secret would be safe forever. But then when he heard Frome's daughter planned to donate her father's artwork to the Comic Art Museum, Rudd was scared out of his wits, and that's when he told me the whole story.

"If someone at the museum discovered that Frome was the real creator of the Apeman," Kelso continued, "not only would Star Comix and the FBS network be exposed to a costly lawsuit— Frome's daughter might even go to court to get 'The Apeman' television show forced off the air until the suit was settled.

"I'd be fired from the network," Kelso told the boys. "My career would be ruined."

Then he had seen the television news film showing the fake Apeman's raid on the Alfresco Disco. He had recognized Rollo Eckert as the impostor and had hired a private detective to track him.

"That's when he started blackmailing me!" Eckert broke in. "He said if I didn't agree to swipe Frome's story from the Comic Art Museum, he'd turn me in to the cops! But if I helped him out, he'd fix it so I could take over the starring role in 'The Apeman' show next season."

"If you believed that, you'll believe anything!" Joe said sarcastically.

"What difference does it make now?" whined Kelso. "Anyhow, my troubles didn't stop there. My houseman-chauffeur got sick, and I needed someone to take his place temporarily . . ."

"So you hired one of the Children of Noah!" said Frank.

"Quite right!" rasped an unexpected voice. "Brilliant detective work, my two young snoops!"

The Hardys whirled at the sound. A bearded man had just entered the cottage!

The boys' faces showed their dismay as they recognized Noah Norvel. With him were four of his armed guards!

# 20

## A Screaming Finish

"Where did you come from?" Joe exclaimed.

"From the Bayport airfield, same as you." The bearded cult leader bared his teeth in a wolfish grin. "You see, I keep a private plane at the Westchester County Airport. That's where I headed as soon as I got rid of the police after you two left. My faithful followers had a car waiting for me when we landed, so we drove straight here to Rollo's cottage. I was quite sure this was where we'd find him and Kelso."

"Wait a minute!" Frank broke in. "Let's go back to that crack you made when you walked in just now. Am I right in thinking you get your cult members to pass on information that they pick up

176

in the households where they work as temporary servants?"

"Of course! No harm in telling you, since you punks will never get a chance to inform the police." Noah boastfully explained that in various big cities along the East Coast his young culties were often hired to do housework and other chores in the homes of important business executives. They were trained to report any interesting items they overheard, in the belief that these might be useful in making the cult's own business investments, and thereby help their great leader Noah "improve the world."

Culties employed in the homes of government officials and diplomats in Washington were trained to do the same thing. "What the fools don't realize," Norvel chuckled, "is that I can sell all those valuable business secrets and security data to foreign buyers overseas."

"Including enemies of your own country," Joe said scornfully.

"It's no skin off my nose how they use the information I sell them," the cult leader sneered.

"Let me guess what else your culties do," said Frank. "You've also trained them to sneak out any valuable jewelry or art objects they happen to spot, so their wonderful leader can have a chance to see and enjoy such examples of fine craftsmanship.

177

What you don't tell them is that the objects you give them back to return to their employers' homes are *forgeries*, while you keep the real items and sell them to underworld fences!"

"Correct!" Again Norvel chuckled wolfishly. "A perfect setup, wouldn't you say? The owners seldom discover the switch, and my youthful stooges don't realize they're being used as thieves!"

Sue Linwood gasped. "You're *disgusting!*" she cried. Joe had removed her gag but had not yet finished untying her from the chair when Noah and his armed guards burst into the cottage. Now her blue eyes blazed at the bearded cult leader. "To think I was foolish enough to become one of your children!"

"But you did, my dear," Norvel rasped, "and what's more, you even helped me dispose of some of the loot. It so happens that the package you delivered to the art dealer's shop in New York contained a stolen painting!"

Sue's face froze in a look of utter dismay.

"You won't get away with the rackets you've been pulling!" Joe snapped.

"If you mean because your father, the great gumshoe Fenton Hardy, is on my trail—that remains to be seen!"

Noah, the Hardy boys now learned, had recently become aware that the famous detective suspected his criminal activities and was trying to collect evidence against him. So he ordered some of his bolder followers, who had already been in trouble with the law before joining his cult, to spy on the Hardy house and to harass the family in every way possible.

One such cultie, by listening at the window, had seen Frank and Joe watching "The Apeman" show on television. He had done the spooky growling and made the huge footprints and later called the police. Other culties had caused the boys' car trouble in Shoreham and had made the threatening phone calls to Mrs. Hardy and Aunt Gertrude. They had also trailed the boys to New York. Because there were enough culties to take turns from time to time, it was difficult for Frank and Joe to notice that any particular person was shadowing them.

The amulet and scrap of paper with the Hardys' address had been dropped by one young spy who tailed them to the disco party. His pocket had been ripped in the bustle and scuffle during the fake Apeman's getaway. But it was Rollo himself who had appeared at the Hardys' window and broken the pane, because he was enraged at Frank and Joe for spoiling his raid on the disco.

Frank suddenly snapped his fingers. "You were also the cripple we saw on the park bench that night!" he exclaimed to Eckert. "You must've changed clothes in the bushes and strapped on your plaster cast. That's how you managed your vanishing act!"

It was also Rollo Eckert, the Hardys now realized, who had attacked Joe outside the Olympic Gym. He had hidden in the phone booth and called the manager's office when he saw the Hardys leaving. Moments later, when Joe was alone in the corridor, it was Rollo's crutch that had struck him from behind.

"But let's get back to this creep," said Frank, turning a contemptuous glance on Noah Norvel again. "The cultie that Kelso hired discovered the art folder—the one that Rollo Eckert had stolen for Kelso from the Comic Art Museum. So the cultie brought it to Noah, and when Noah went through it he spotted Archie Frome's original Apeman cartoons and realized Star Comix must have stolen the character. With the cartoons for evidence, he knew he could make Star and the television producers pay him plenty not to spill the beans."

"But Kelso had a trick up his sleeve, too," said Joe. "When Noah tried to blackmail him, he sent Rollo to Noah's mansion tonight to get back the evidence!"

"Brilliant, as I've said before," the cult leader sneered. "But we're wasting time."

"You'll be wasting a lot more behind bars," Frank snapped, "when the truth comes out!"

"Then I'd better make sure it doesn't, hadn't I?" Noah Norvel chuckled nastily. "Which shouldn't be too hard once this cottage burns down, with all of you inside it! . . . All right, torch the place!" he added, turning to his four guards.

Meanwhile, Joe had whispered something hastily to Sue Linwood. Suddenly she began to scream at the top of her lungs.

"Shut her up!" Noah shouted angrily to his men. "If that racket carries far enough, she'll have every cottage on the beach wakened up before this place is even set on fire!"

One of the guards darted toward her and tried to clap his hand over her mouth. But Sue writhed away from him and kept on screaming!

With all of the crooks' attention focused on the girl, Frank and Joe seized their chance to fight back. Joe grabbed a chair and disarmed one guard, while Frank floored another with a hard left to the jaw!

Vern Kelso and Rollo Eckert quickly joined in the fray. In moments, the scene in the cottage turned to bedlam as Noah's party fought wildly with their intended victims. The furniture was smashed. At one point, Rollo picked up one guard bodily and hurled him clear across the front room!

But above the noise, the Hardy boys heard the roar of an engine as a plane swooped down toward the beach. Scarcely a minute or two later, three men came charging in the front door of the cottage. Fenton Hardy was in the lead, followed by Jack Wayne and Zack Amboy!

The tide of the battle soon turned, and the famed private investigator now took charge of the prisoners. Not only were Noah Norvel and his guards lined up with their hands in the air and their faces to the wall, but Vern Kelso and Rollo Eckert were as well.

"You'll all answer to the law!" Mr. Hardy told them curtly. "Great work, Sons!" he added proudly to Frank and Joe. "You not only solved your own cases, but mine, too!"

The boys learned that soon after his first radio contact with Jack Wayne, he had found a pilot willing to fly him from Long Island to the Westchester County Airport, where Wayne and Zack Amboy had picked him up after dropping the boys at Bayport.

Further questioning revealed that Micky Rudd, aside from pirating Archie Frome's cartoon character, had not taken part in the network executive's violent attempts to cover up the secret.

"Did Kelso drug Zack Amboy?" Joe asked.

"He had Rollo Eckert do it and tried to frame Zack by means of the two anonymous phone calls and the drawing dropped in the museum," Mr. Hardy replied.

Frank shook his head. "And all this to keep his job," he said.

"I'm afraid the network will have to get along without him from now on," Mr. Hardy said with a grin. "He'll be in prison for a long time!"

After the criminals had been delivered to the police, the Hardy boys went home, dead tired. Just before he fell asleep, Frank vaguely wondered if there would be another mystery for them to solve in the future. But he was too exhausted to worry about it and had no idea that *The Mummy Case* would soon require their full attention.

The Hardy boys were awakened the next morning by a visit from Chet Morton. The fat boy looked utterly crestfallen as he showed them a set of photostats he had just received in the mail from Star Comix. The photostats showed how his Captain Muscles story would look when published in one of the Star Comix books.

"Just look what they've done!" Chet wailed. "They've changed the wording in the balloons to make Captain Muscles sound like an idiot! They're running it as a *funny* story, as if the whole thing's a joke!"

"Well, after all, it'll appear in a *comic* book," Joe pointed out, smothering a grin.

"Never mind him, Chet," Frank sympathized,

clapping the double-chinned cartoonist on the back. "Besides, you've still got the money they're paying you. That ought to be good for *some* fun!"

"You're right," said the fat boy, brightening up as his usual good humor came to the surface again. "Tell you what, guys! I'll use it to throw another big disco party for all the Bayport gang!"

You are invited to join

THE OFFICIAL
HARDY BOYS® FAN CLUB!

Be the first in your neighborhood to find out about Frank and Joe's newest adventures in the *Hardy Boys ® Mystery Reporter,* and to receive your official membership card. Just send your name, age, address, and zip code to:

**The Official Hardy Boys® Fan Club**
**Wanderer Books**
**1230 Avenue of the Americas**
**New York, NY 10020**

## Don't miss these new mystery stories

THE HARDY BOYS® 59
Night of the Werewolf
by Franklin W. Dixon

THE HARDY BOYS® 60
Mystery of the Samurai
    Sword
by Franklin W. Dixon

THE HARDY BOYS® 61
The Pentagon Spy
by Franklin W. Dixon

NANCY DREW® 57
The Triple Hoax
by Carolyn Keene

NANCY DREW® 58
The Flying Saucer
    Mystery
by Carolyn Keene

## Plus exciting survival stories in

The Hardy Boys® Handbook
Seven Stories Of Survival
by Franklin W. Dixon
with Sheila Link

*Available in Wanderer Paperback and
Wanderer Reinforced Editions*